His lips demanded a response.

Firm, yet soft, Sean's mouth came down on hers. Incredible warmth filled Annie's chest. She'd been cold for so long. But now she felt safe. She started to push against his chest, but he pulled her closer and deepened the kiss. A moan bubbled up inside her throat that seemed to ignite his desire even more. With one arm wrapped her waist, the other pulled her against him as if he couldn't get enough.

She couldn't fight this. A memory flashed to the surface, as if they'd done this before. And it felt so right.

Sean broke the kiss and her mind swam in confusion. Tipping her head back, she studied his dark green eyes and saw layers of raw pain that made her own chest ache. There was more to this man than the images in her scattered memory. Much more.

"Now *that,* I remember," Annie said, softly.

PAT WHITE

SILENT MEMORIES

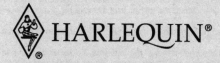

HARLEQUIN®

TORONTO • NEW YORK • LONDON
AMSTERDAM • PARIS • SYDNEY • HAMBURG
STOCKHOLM • ATHENS • TOKYO • MILAN • MADRID
PRAGUE • WARSAW • BUDAPEST • AUCKLAND

Thanks to Debra Webb for opening the door,
and Denise Zaza for inviting me in.

ISBN-13: 978-0-373-22944-4
ISBN-10:   0-373-22944-5

SILENT MEMORIES

Copyright: © 2006 by Pat White

This edition published by arrangement with Harlequin Books S.A.

www.eHarlequin.com

Printed in U.S.A.

ABOUT THE AUTHOR

Growing up in the Midwest, Pat White has been spinning stories in her head ever since she was a little girl, stories filled with mystery, romance and adventure. Years later, while trying to solve the mysteries of raising a family in a house full of men, she started writing romantic fiction. After six Golden Heart nominations and a *Romantic Times BOOKclub* Award for Best Contemporary Romance (2004), her passion for storytelling and love of a good romance continues to find a voice in her tales of romantic suspense. Pat now lives in the Pacific Northwest and she's still trying to solve the mysteries of living in a house full of men—with the added complication of two silly dogs and three spoiled cats. She loves to hear from readers, so please visit her at www.patwhitebooks.com.

Books by Pat White

CAST OF CHARACTERS

Sean MacNeil—Undercover FBI agent assigned to protect naive scientist Annie Price, not fall in love with her.

Annie Price—Sheltered scientist who awakens after a coma with no memory yet she senses that Sean is responsible for the car accident that nearly killed her.

Raymond Phelps—Millionaire who took Annie into his home as his protégée, giving her the education she needed to develop her brilliant mind. But are his motivations genuine or sinister?

Chapter One

Sean MacNeil gripped the steering wheel of his Ford Explorer and stared out the front windshield at the aging building. Ivy climbed up the side of the red brick, stretching and curling, reaching out for life.

But inside there was no life. Only souls passing time until they reached their next stop, empty minds content in mindlessness.

The windshield wipers stroked away the rain, now coming in torrents over the New England countryside. He wished that just for today he could forget who he was, who she was. That just for today, he could go to a ball game or movie without thinking of her. She'd never know the difference. She lived in a land of contentment sitting in her corner, rocking, humming, shutting out everything that happened before last spring, when deception had obliterated her calm, happy life.

The chain grew heavy around his soul; the only relief was his obligatory visit. Except for this past month, he'd done his weekly chore. He'd driven out to the remote hospital and checked on the patient they'd named Mary, the woman he knew as someone else.

If only he could rid himself of this curse. But some mistakes were eternal ones. And "Mary" was his.

The rhythmic swish of the wipers calmed him somehow, the frantic pace of his heart slowing to a steady beat. The rain was letting up. Maybe he'd spot a rainbow or two before the day was out.

He swung open the door and stepped onto the slick asphalt, hesitating before he made the twenty-yard trek to the front door. The staff would be pleased that someone cared enough to visit. A nurse would lead him to Mary's room, where he'd find the twenty-seven-year-old woman huddled in a corner, her fingers wrapped around a tattered stuffed animal. A rabbit? A dog? He wasn't sure. He'd never gotten that close.

Flipping his raincoat collar to shield his neck, he vaulted the brick stairs two at a time. He reached the landing and gave his head a shake, ridding his hair of excess moisture.

He knocked on the door. Paced. Waited. Knocked again. Damn, he wanted this over. He wanted to perform his duty, turn tail and race the two hundred miles back to the City.

"One moment please," a voice said through the intercom.

He glanced over his shoulder at the Maine country-side. Trees glowed yellow, orange and red with the coming of fall. Peaceful. That's what he hated about the country. It promised something he knew didn't exist.

His gaze drifted down to his black high-tops, remembering a time when the shine on his shoes was more important than his next meal.

The front door creaked open. Nurse Redmond greeted him with a scowl, her face pale, her gray hair pulled back into a taut bun.

"Mr. MacNeil, we haven't seen you in a while." She escorted him to the main desk where he scribbled his name in the visitors' log.

"I've been out of town on business," he said.

"Mary will be happy to see you."

Happy? Mary? Hell, she didn't know where she was, who Sean was. "If you say so."

"You must have faith," Nurse Redmond said. "I've worked in many hospitals and have seen some amazing things. Miracles can happen."

Her eyes were so round and serious. He couldn't laugh, not in the woman's face. Let her float in her bubble of fantasy. Let someone still believe in miracles.

"I'd like to see Mary," he said.

She pursed her lips and led him down the hall to the north wing.

He ignored the cries of patients that echoed down the barren white hallway. Every time he left this place the hollowness of their cries haunted him at night, waking him with their agony. Nurse Redmond greeted another, younger nurse.

"Lydia. This is Mr. MacNeil. Could you take him the rest of the way? I have to check on Mrs. Banks."

"Sure."

Nurse Redmond avoided eye contact with Sean. She lifted her chin and marched down the hall, disappearing into a room.

Contempt. That's the weapon she'd aimed at him. Contempt for not believing in miracles.

The same expression that stared back at him every day he looked in the mirror.

"Mr. MacNeil?"

He turned his attention to Nurse Lydia. Young and fresh, like Mary probably looked ten years ago.

"Are you okay?" she asked.

He shoved his hands into his raincoat pockets. "Just tired."

Tired of life. Tired of death. Tired of serving a sentence he didn't deserve.

She smiled and led him down the hall toward his "wife's" room. He followed slowly, struggling with each step. God, why hadn't he listened to Connors? Why hadn't he stuck with the original plan instead of improvising one of his own? What had he been thinking?

That's the point. He hadn't used his brain; he'd acted from the heart. Never again.

"Will you be coming back Saturday?" the young nurse asked.

"Saturday?"

"We have a special variety show planned."

"Today is the only day I can make it." *The only day I can muster the emotional strength.*

They turned the corner to Mary's room. "That's a shame. It's a great show."

Great for whom? Not for Sean, who fought back an inferno of pain each time he visited his "wife" and knew that *he* was to blame for her condition.

"Mary's the star of the show," the nurse continued.

"She doesn't even know where she is."

"Maybe not. But she knows she's going to be in the show. She's very exited about it. She told me herself."

She told me herself. Impossible.

He touched the sleeve of her white polyester uniform. "What did you say?"

She glanced over her shoulder at him. "I said, Mary told me she was excited about performing."

"Mary hasn't spoken in nearly six months."

"We've made great progress in the last month. Dr. Zinkerman's new drug has done wonders. Mary can even write her name." She opened the door and he followed her inside. "Can't you, Mary?"

He glanced across the room. The woman they'd named Mary sat in her rocking chair, staring out the window as she had so many times during his visits.

Only this time, she turned at the sound of the nurse's voice.

Something was different. They'd cut her hair, feathered it back about her face like she'd worn it as a teenager. Her shirt didn't list off her shoulder, her cheeks were more pinkish than white. She looked almost normal. He absently took a step back, bracing himself against the wall for support.

"Mary?" Nurse Lydia said.

The sound of Nurse Lydia's voice put Mary at ease. Nurse Lydia was kind and helpful, and today she'd even brought a visitor. Maybe it was someone who could tell her who she was and where she'd come from. She put her glasses to the bridge of her nose to get a better look.

Her heart stopped cold and she choked on rising panic.

Oh God, no. Not him.

"Mary? What's wrong?" Nurse Lydia asked.

She couldn't speak, her voice frozen in her chest.

Rain slapping the car window; tears streaming down her face. Blinded by bright lights...coming toward her...jerk the wheel. Her breath torn from her chest.

"Nooo," she moaned. Voice—her own voice. Speaking, pleading.

Get him out of here, she wanted to cry. Out of her room. She didn't want to crash, didn't want to get hurt again.

"Gooooo!" she cried. They'd have to make him leave, wouldn't they? They wouldn't force her to be with him in the same room, alone. She'd just learned to use her mouth, her tongue, to form words. She couldn't use it before, afraid of what would come out. That sound. The shrill screech that rang in her ears. Her piercing cry for help.

She gasped for air, but her throat constricted. Stars danced before her eyes. She struggled to focus on the picture across the room. It showed an enchanted castle on a mountain. That's where she belonged. Not here, surrounded by sick people. She grabbed her throat, willed it to relax, to open up. Her eyes watered and her mouth went dry.

"Help me get her on the bed!" Nurse Lydia said.

No. He'd touch her. He'd hurt her again.

"Noooo," she cried, using her last breath to fend off the monster who stood motionless in the corner of her room. She knew she was weak. Vulnerable and at a disadvantage. But that wouldn't stop her from fighting.

"Station One, we need a doctor up here, right away," Nurse Lydia called into the intercom.

Mary curled her fingers tighter around the arms of the metal chair. The man stepped closer.

"It's okay, Mary. You'll be okay." The nurse approached her.

Mary couldn't take her eyes off the huge man dressed in black, eyes like ice.

"Go to her." Lydia motioned to the man.

No, not him!

He took a step. Then another. He didn't look as if he wanted to help. Of course he didn't. He wanted her dead. He crouched in front of her. She clenched the arms of the chair for strength. What would he do? Strangle her? Right here in front of Nurse Lydia?

She looked away, searched over his shoulder for Nurse Lydia's calming eyes and warm smile. The man cupped her chin with his forefinger and thumb and guided her gaze back to his dark, icy stare. She closed her eyes, not wanting her last image on earth to be those cruel, green eyes. She struggled to inhale air through her nose. Nothing worked. Everything broken. Her leg, her hip, her heart.

"Please, open your eyes."

That voice. Smooth as silk, deep as the ocean, and she was drowning in it. God, help her. Take the devil from her room and rescue her from hell.

"I'm not going to hurt you."

Liar. She was already hurt. Her bones ached when it rained. Her mind had been pulverized until a few weeks ago. Thanks to him.

She wouldn't give up, wouldn't lose the precious gift she'd been given: her life. She sucked in air between her teeth, her brain needing oxygen to keep from shutting down completely.

"Do you know who I am?" He touched her forearm.

Won't somebody help me? Warmth crept up her arm. Heat, red-hot, like fire.

"Nooo!" Her eyes shot open and she shoved at his chest. He fell backward and she jumped to her feet, pain shooting down her left side. The rain. The ache. She crossed the room, her hands clutching her hip.

"Mary, calm down." Nurse Lydia reached for her. "Surely you remember your husband, Sean?"

Husband? It couldn't be. That meant he'd cared for her, touched her. This man, this monster who wanted her dead.

She pushed Nurse Lydia aside, stumbled toward the door and collided with Dr. Zinkerman.

"What's all this?" The doctor's firm hands shackled her upper arms. "You're upset."

Damn straight she was upset. She was fighting for her life.

"No…husband." She pointed to the man sitting on the floor. The devil looked dumbstruck, as if he couldn't believe she'd unmasked his true identity.

"It's a shock." Dr. Zinkerman steered her to the bed. She gripped his white coat, scrunching the starched cotton between her fingers. She wouldn't let go, not as long as the devil hovered close by.

"Lie down and we'll give you something to help you relax."

She didn't want to relax, she didn't want to float away over the rolling hills like she did whenever he gave her the shot. She had finally awakened. There was too much to do, to see, to feel.

To finally feel.

"No…sleep," she protested.

"Mary, I always do what's best for you, don't I?" The doctor nodded over his shoulder at the nurse. Mary's focus shot to the devil, who hadn't moved from his spot on the floor. She heard rattling behind the doctor. The shot. They were giving it to her whether she liked it or not.

"No sleep!" she cried, in case Dr. Zinkerman hadn't understood her the first time.

"No sleep, Mary. Just something to calm you down. You're excited. It's been too much for you in one day."

He coaxed her head to the pillow and she stared into his light brown eyes. Gentle eyes. She trusted him to take care of her. He wouldn't let the devil hurt her again. But what if she was the only one who knew the devil's true identity?

"Gooo!" She pointed at the devil.

"Get him out of here," Dr. Zinkerman ordered.

The devil didn't budge.

"Please, let's go outside and give the doctor some time." Nurse Lydia touched his shoulder.

Sean's gaze drifted to the nurse. He felt as if he were in a dream, but it wasn't one of his usual nightmares where they'd found her, tortured and killed her.

"Please, Mr. MacNeil," the nurse pleaded.

"Right." He got to his feet, not taking his eyes off the doctor.

"I'll be outside," he said, clarifying that he wasn't leaving until he got answers about her condition. Was this temporary? Permanent? Did she know who she was? Who he was? Hell, for her sake he hoped not.

The nurse led him to the door. He glanced over his shoulder once, catching the relief that blanketed Mary's face. She looked at the doctor with such trust. Sean's gut clenched.

Of course she trusted the doctor. The doctor hadn't betrayed her in the worst way. Good ol' Sean. Smart, clever Sean. Hell, if he was that smart, she wouldn't have ended up in a place like this, her mind obliterated by the carnage.

Pushing through the door, he slammed his fist against the wall outside her room. "Damn it!"

"I'm sorry."

He turned and studied the young nurse whose round face strained with sympathy.

"I really thought she'd be happy to see you. She gets confused sometimes."

He forced a smile. An ally would be good right about now. "I don't understand. The last time I saw her, she was, you know…"

"Noncommunicative."

He nodded, his thoughts spinning like a top. What next? Should he call the Bureau? Tell them she'd awakened? What would they do with her?

"It was a combination of things that brought her around." The nurse led him toward a waiting area. "The new medication helped, plus Dr. Zinkerman has been spending extra time with her."

She motioned for him to sit on the gray vinyl couch. Nurse Lydia sat in the high-backed chair. "We're so glad to have Dr. Zinkerman with us."

"I don't remember him being on staff before."

"He joined us a few months ago. He started working with Mary only recently."

New. Recent. He gripped the arm of the couch. He'd been successful in keeping her identity a secret so far, keeping her safe and protected. No one could have traced her here. Unless—

He jumped to his feet and paced the small waiting area. He was too savvy an agent to believe in complete safety. Hell, he'd seen it all, from businessmen who moonlighted as drug dealers to wealthy aristocrats who manipulated children away from their families. Innocent, defenseless children. He balled his hand into a fist.

"Mr. MacNeil? Are you all right?" the nurse asked.

"Yep," he lied.

"She'll come around. You've got to believe that."

"Thanks for trying to make me feel better." His gaze drifted to the floor.

"Things will work out." She got up and touched his arm.

He felt no warmth from her touch. Not like he had when he'd touched Mary's pale skin. He wanted to rub his fingers across the back of her hand until she calmed down. It reminded him of sweeter, happier times.

Just now, he'd read panic in her eyes. Yet he was

the only man who could protect her. He would protect her, damn it, even if it killed him.

"Everything will work out. Dr. Zinkerman is wonderful," Nurse Lydia offered.

Zinkerman, the mystery doctor who happened to join the staff a few months ago. Sean bottled up his emotions.

"Tell me about the doctor." He sat down on the sofa.

Nurse Lydia smiled, seemingly pleased that she'd distracted him from his own misery. "Dr. Zinkerman has excellent credentials and keeps on top of the latest breakthroughs in drug therapy. Mary couldn't be in better hands."

"Where's he from?" He rubbed the back of his neck.

"He's a University of Chicago graduate. He worked in a research facility in Oregon."

Oregon. He tensed.

"There you are," Dr. Zinkerman said, coming toward them. The fiftyish, balding man slipped a pen into his lab coat pocket. He walked up to Sean and extended his hand. Sean stood.

"I wish we could have met under better circumstances, Mr. MacNeil. I'm sorry about what happened back there."

Sean stared hard into the man's eyes. Looking for what? Answers to his true motivation? Who was he kidding?

"I'm a bit confused, Doctor. The last time I visited

Mary, she was noncommunicative. Today there's a different woman sitting there."

"It's fantastic, isn't it?"

"I wouldn't exactly call what happened back there fantastic." He settled on the padded couch, his mind swimming in possibilities.

Dr. Zinkerman sat across the coffee table from him. He glanced at the nurse. "Thank you, Nurse."

Nurse Lydia smiled at Sean, then disappeared down the hall.

"I'm a bit concerned about her reaction to you," the doctor said. "I thought she'd be happy. Instead, the level of anxiety has caused me to reevaluate my initial recommendation."

"Which was?"

"To let her go home, to be with her family as soon as possible."

Sean sucked in a sharp breath. There was no home, no family, for his patient to return to. He couldn't take her to his apartment, a pit buried in the heart of Boston.

"After seeing her reaction today, I'm afraid releasing her is out of the question," the doctor said. "She'll have to stay at Appleton until I'm convinced she's not at risk."

"And how long will that be?"

"As long as it takes." The doctor leaned forward, his brown eyes narrow with concern. "I can't chance her regaining her senses only to have an emotional breakdown. It could do irreparable damage. No, I think the best thing is to let her stay with us until she shows a desire to go home with you."

Hell would freeze over before that would happen. He studied the doctor, wondering who he really was and if he wanted the best for her. It was about time someone did.

Sean stood, acting the part of pained husband. "This is all a bit overwhelming. She seems almost normal today after months of being out of it. Yet you're telling me I can't take her home?"

"You saw her in there, Mr. MacNeil. She's in no condition to go anywhere with you."

"I'm her husband." His chest ached with the lie.

"I understand that, sir. But we have to think about Mary."

Think about Mary. All Sean had done for the past six months was think about "Mary."

"What are you suggesting?" Sean said.

"We're working with her on basic skills: feeding herself, clothing herself. She's come a long way. She's learned to write. We've encouraged her to keep a journal of memories. They come back to her in flashes."

Memories. The past. The horror. That could send anyone over the edge.

"Will she remember everything?" He needed to know the severity of the situation.

"It's possible. No one knows for sure."

"This drug the nurse told me about, is that what's caused her recovery?"

"Partially. We also noticed a reduction in swelling around the brain on her most recent MRI."

"And if she's taken off the medication?"

"That won't happen. Not as long as she's in my care."

Dr. Zinkerman stood and extended his hand. "It would be nice if you could visit more than once a week. I think she just needs to get used to you again."

Sean glanced out the window. The rain had stopped.

"Would you like to set up a visit for next Tuesday?" Zinkerman suggested. "We could discuss a permanent plan for your wife, maybe move her to the east wing if you'd like. It's for patients who are physically challenged. It's our long-term facility."

Long-term. Was that for her benefit or Zinkerman's? He studied the doctor's concerned expression. He'd been so good at reading people's faces once, guessing their thoughts. This man revealed nothing through his deep-set eyes and rehearsed smile.

"I'll look forward to seeing you next week, then?" Zinkerman said.

Next week might be too late.

"Thank you, Doctor." He shook the man's hand, glancing down for a split second. He noticed a wide, pale band of skin on his right ring finger. He glanced at Zinkerman's shoes. They shined brighter than a freshly minted coin.

He released Zinkerman's hand and shot him a pleasant smile. A smile convincing the man who called himself a doctor that Sean had bought the garbage he was peddling. Sure, Mary was in good hands.

Like hell she was.

"Until next week." Sean nodded and walked toward the main entrance. He slowed his pace when he passed Mary's room and felt the doctor's eyes bore a hole through his back. Zinkerman didn't want anything or anyone interfering with his patient. Of course not. Zinkerman, or whoever he was, had direct access to the world's salvation—or destruction. That's why he kept an extra close watch over her and encouraged her to write in a journal.

He stopped at the front desk, scribbled his name in the visitors' book, then glanced down the hall. She thought Sean the enemy and Dr. Zinkerman her savior.

If she only knew.

Heading for the parking lot, he wondered how long she'd remain coherent. Long enough to accidentally spill the whole story to a nurse? Write formulas in her diary? He made his way to his truck, got behind the wheel and sized up the building. One of the reasons he'd picked this place was because of its high security, the same security that would work against him tonight.

He knew what he had to do. She wasn't safe anymore. But then, neither was anyone else.

Chapter Two

She awakened with a start, engulfed in darkness.

"Scream and you're dead," a voice threatened in her ear. Pressure against her neck pinned her cheek to the starched pillowcase of the hospital bed.

It was the devil, back to finish what he'd started. He saw how weak she was, how fragile.

Breathe. I have to breathe.

The devil slid black material over her head and pulled it snug around her throat. He flipped her onto her back. Oh, God. This was it. He was going to kill her.

Like a feral animal, she swung her arms and kicked her legs in the hopes of hitting something crucial. A large, stiff hand clamped against her throat. Clutching his arm, she dug her fingers into taut muscle.

"Stop fighting or I'll finish this." His hard, brutal voice was nothing like the seductive tone he'd used during his visit earlier.

She pulled on his wrists to loosen his grip—had to get air.

"You gonna keep quiet?"

She stilled, stars flickering across the backs of her eyelids. He released her and she gasped, sucking much needed air through the thick fabric. A ripping sound sent shivers up her spine. Her wrists were clamped together and bound.

"Keep your mouth shut until we're out of here." He smacked her upside the head. Tears stung her eyes.

In a swift motion, he had her up and over his shoulder. She didn't stand a chance against this beast. He dumped her into a receptacle, her body sinking into the soft mass of what she guessed was bed linen. The devil rolled the container across the vinyl floor.

Squeak…squeak, groaned a wheel.

Help me! Somebody help me!

"Excuse me."

She recognized the doctor's voice. Thank God. If only she could cry out, Dr. Zinkerman would save her!

"Yes, Doctor," the devil said.

Why didn't the doctor question the man who claimed to be her husband? Was he wearing a disguise?

She swallowed hard, pressed her tongue against the roof of her mouth to form sounds. Nothing happened. Panic strangled her vocal cords.

"Did you get *all* the laundry?" Dr. Zinkerman said.

"Yes, sir."

Laundry. No, not laundry. I'm in here. I'm being dragged away from my bed by a man who plans to kill me.

"Doc-tor," she groaned.

Silence filled the hallway.

"Doc-tor."

Why didn't the doctor pull back the sheets to investigate?

"Get her out of here," Dr. Zinkerman ordered.

Her blood ran cold.

"Give her something to shut her up," her kidnapper demanded.

She curled up into a ball, anticipating the prick that would render her unconscious. She couldn't let them drug her, couldn't pass out and wake up…where? Six feet under?

God had given her another chance at life, and she wasn't about to let the devil rob her of it.

She sprung from her fetal position and toppled the cart. Burrowing out from under the laundry, she crawled on her belly across the vinyl floor. Strong hands grabbed her by the shoulders and pinned her against the wall. Her cheek smacked it dead-on. With numb fingers, she slid the sack from her head and gulped air like an asthmatic.

"Let me handle this," Dr. Zinkerman said. "Wait downstairs." Footsteps echoed toward her.

"Mary?" the good doctor said sweetly. She turned and struggled to focus against the fluorescent lights. He came toward her, his arms extended, palms up in a comforting gesture.

"Everything's okay, Mary," he assured.

Everything was definitely not okay. She scanned the hallway. The devil was nowhere in sight.

"Let's get you back to your room," Dr. Zinkerman said.

He didn't offer to untie her wrists. He hadn't done a damn thing to help her when the devil had tossed her against the wall. She blinked back tears of frustration and inched away from the doctor.

"Mary, please. I wouldn't want to have to put you in restraints."

Restraints. Immobile. Helpless. Vulnerable to a man who wanted to kill her.

Zinkerman took a step closer. She spotted a syringe pinched between his freshly manicured fingers.

"Mary, you've always trusted me," he said.

She'd play along, for the moment. But there was no way in hell she'd believe a word uttered by this man.

"I want to give you some medication to help you relax. I know things are confusing. But when you wake up it will all be clear."

He took two steps, three, four. She knew damn well that if he injected her, she *wouldn't* live to regret it. He backed her into a short hallway, leading to an office. She spun around and pulled at the door, but it was locked.

"Life is confusing sometimes," he continued.

She turned back to him, trapped.

"Things aren't always what they appear to be," he said.

Like you, she wanted to scream.

"I think once you sleep, you'll feel much better."

He reached for her arm, but didn't remove the duct tape from her wrists. She glanced into his soft brown eyes. A tinge of evil sparkled back at her.

With a lunge and a cry, she bit into his forearm. He swore and dropped the syringe. She started to run, but he tripped her and she fell to the floor, only inches from the syringe.

"It's best if you cooperate," he said from behind her.

She fingered the syringe, slipping it between her palms. In one, swift motion, he pulled her to her feet and she stabbed him with the needle.

"Ah!" He stumbled against the wall.

"Your only chance was with me," he said. "He'll…kill you."

Sliding down the wall, he fell limp onto his side, eyes partially open. With frantic breaths, she ripped his keys from his belt. She peeked around the corner into the main hallway and spotted a fire alarm. Padding quietly across the hall, she broke the protective shield and set off the alarm.

The high-pitched squeal pinched her ears. Doors opened. Lights flashed. She had to get out of here before the devil returned.

Doctors shouted orders, nurses and orderlies raced from room to room. In the chaos, no one noticed that her hands were bound.

Staff members herded patients to safety, but Mary

couldn't go with them. The devil would surely search there first.

Pushing through the swarm of sleepy, sweaty bodies, she struggled to get to the opposite exit. Her mind raced. Where would she go once she left this place? She didn't even know where she was, or who she was.

But she did know she would refuse to die at the hands of a murderer.

She bolted through the door, conscious of the killer still on the grounds who was determined to find her. Her hip ached and the skin on her wrists rubbed raw from the duct tape. She managed a lopsided sprint across the parking lot to the garden. Angry raindrops pelted her cheeks and arms, and soaked through her lightweight pajamas. The wet fabric clung to her body like wet tissue paper.

The devil was near. She could feel him. Damn her legs for not moving faster. Damn her heart for trusting Zinkerman and believing she was safe.

She dove into the bushes for cover, scrambling deeper into the mass of green. Her hands met with cold metal—a steel fence. She'd never been out this far, never knew what really held them prisoners. Her heart sank. The devil would surely find her now.

"Do you want to live?"

She jumped at the sound of a man's voice from the opposite side of the fence. All she could see was darkness.

"Where are you, darlin'?" echoed the voice of the man who had ripped her from her bed. He now stalked her from the perimeter of the bushes.

"Come out, come out wherever you are," he sang.

She curled her fingers around the fence, desperate to see the face of the man who claimed to offer her life.

"Come on, crazy lady. I'm not going to hurt you," the devil promised.

The swish of leaves shot panic across her shoulders. He was coming for her. He wouldn't give up. Her only chance was accepting help from the faceless stranger.

An apparition suddenly appeared on the opposite side of the woven metal. His black-gloved hands pulled at the bottom of the fence. Black covered his entire body from his ski mask to his boots. His corded arm muscles strained through the tight knit shirt as he stretched the fence to allow her through.

"I didn't want to do this, crazy lady," the man called from behind her.

Pop. Pop. A bullet smacked the wet earth beside her. If she stayed here, she was dead for sure.

She searched her rescuer's face.

"I guess I gotta come get you," her pursuer said.

She leaned closer to the fence. If only he'd look at her so she could get a glimpse of—

He glanced up and her heart stopped. The darkest shade of green stared back at her.

It couldn't be! The devil who claimed to be her husband this afternoon, then dragged her from her bed just now? She thought he was the man shooting at her. Instead he was here, holding the fence open.

Then who was shooting at her?

"C'mon." The man named Sean pulled on the fence to give her more space.

She couldn't believe he was the one who beckoned her to hell with the promise of life.

"I don't want to get my clothes dirty, crazy lady. So I'll keep shootin' until I know you're dead. That okay with you?" the voice said from behind her.

Pop. Pop.

She could have sworn a bullet whizzed by her ear. She had two choices: death or death.

"He *will* kill you," Sean whispered from the other side of the fence.

And you won't? She gritted her teeth and glared at him.

"Give me your hand," he implored.

Give me your soul, she heard.

Pop. Pop.

"Did I get you yet, crazy lady?"

She had to live. And not just for herself. Somehow, she sensed others depended on her.

Sean stuck a leather-gloved hand through the fence. She tore her gaze from his eyes, uncurled her fingers from the cool, steel fence and placed her hand in his palm. He pulled her through and cut the duct tape from her wrists. She rubbed the raw skin.

"Lady, you still in there?"

Shoving her into a crouched position, Sean pressed his index finger to his mouth.

"This is your last chance, crazy lady. Come out and I won't shoot, promise."

With a jerk of his right hand, Sean motioned for her to stay down and start running. The crouched run shot spears of pain down her leg.

Pop. Pop.

Sean grunted and shoved her forward. "Keep running. Follow the markers to the car and wait there."

Wait for you? Are you crazy?

She followed the yellow tags hanging from tree branches. Twigs and pebbles pricked her bare feet. A chill raced through her from the cold rain soaking her pajamas. She struggled to sort out her enemies from her allies. Nothing made sense. Dr. Zinkerman an enemy? The devil her savior?

She pushed through a mass of brush and stumbled toward the car. She slipped on the wet earth and she went down, gray muck splattering her pajama-clad body. Pushing to her feet, she hobbled to the car and locked herself inside.

Where was Sean? What would he do when he got to the car? She fingered the ignition. No keys. She searched the visor, glove compartment, under the seat. Nothing.

There had to be another way to start the car.

You're smart. You can do anything.

She ran her hands down the steering column,

searching for a way in, a way to get a hold of the wires that would spark her chance at freedom.

The car doors unlocked with a deafening click and the driver's door opened.

"Move over," Sean said.

She scooted as far away from him as possible without jumping from the car. Where would she go in the middle of a thunderstorm with no clothes, money or mind to guide her?

He tossed the ski mask into the backseat and pulled away from the shoulder of the deserted road. Her head snapped back against the seat.

"Were you hit?" he asked, concern lacing his voice.

She studied his hard profile, square jaw clenched tight, eyes narrowed to make out the road between sheets of rain. It couldn't be. He couldn't care about her.

"Say something, nod, anything," he said.

Sean squeezed the steering wheel, his leg throbbing from the bullet that had grazed his thigh. The injury wasn't nearly as painful as the thought of the old man getting his hands on her. Or had someone else discovered her location? Someone who was after her formula?

He jammed his foot to the accelerator, anxious to get far away from the evil that nearly had taken her from him for good.

Yeah, like she was ever yours to begin with.

He glanced at his passenger, her eyes wide, her arms wrapped around her midsection. She stared at him with such hatred and distrust.

"Please tell me you're not hurt."

She nodded and hugged herself tighter.

"I'll get you some dry clothes later, but first we need to get as far away from Appleton as we can. Do you understand? That man will probably come looking for you. We can't let him find you. Do you understand?"

He rambled like an idiot, not knowing what else to do. He wasn't sure if she was mentally all there or not, if she understood a word he said. He sped down the Maine farm road toward the sea, knowing if he got her on his sailboat, the *Minerva*, she'd be safe for the time being. That had been the plan: keep her on the boat until it was safe to bring her in. He'd also rented a cabin as a backup.

He would make sure she was safe. He owed her that. Then he would run like hell.

"Who...are you?" she said.

Her voice, rough with lack of use, touched his heart. How many months had he hidden in the shadows of her hospital room aching to hear the sweet sound of her voice? Willing her to open her eyes and forgive him? How many months had he prayed that someday she would even tell him she loved him?

Fool.

"My name is Sean. I knew you before the accident. Do you remember the accident?"

She chewed on her lower lip. He figured she remembered something.

"You were in a coma," he said. "You woke up but were still out of it. You couldn't speak. That's why they moved you to Appleton."

"Husband?" she croaked, pointing her finger at him.

"No, I'm not really your husband."

She closed her eyes and sighed with relief.

His heart sliced in two.

"You're in danger," he said, getting a grip on his emotions.

Her eyes shot open and raked across his body. Heat pooled in his gut.

"No, not from me. I'm going to help you."

The disbelief in her eyes slapped him with shame—had he helped her by making her fall in love with him? Using her, like the rest of the world?

Damn, he should have demanded a transfer months ago.

"Where…?" she asked.

"We're going to my sailboat. We'll be safe there. And mobile."

Getting out to the *Minerva* without being noticed would be a trick. In their present state, they stuck out like two thieves on the run: Sean dressed in black, blood oozing down his leg, his companion dressed in mud-covered pajamas. Wet pajamas that clung to her like a second skin. Not that there was much to cling to. She used to complain about her weight, but Sean thought she was just right—round and voluptuous and incredibly sexy.

He glanced at her. Her ribs poked through the starched cotton of her pajamas; her cheekbones were more pronounced than six months ago.

"Didn't they feed you at that place?" he said, unable to keep the anger from his voice.

Her blue eyes widened and she wrapped her arms tighter around her middle.

"Aw, hell, I'm not mad at you."

He reached out to touch her shoulder. She glared at his hand and he withdrew it. Just as well. He didn't want any confusion about their roles this time around.

"We should change before we get to the harbor. I don't want to draw attention to ourselves. I brought some clothes."

They drove in silence for what seemed like eternity. This was his penance: protecting the woman he loved, the same woman who thought he was the enemy. In reality, wasn't he?

"There, a gas station," he said more to himself than his companion. "We'll use the bathroom to wash up and change."

He parked the car behind the station, got the backpack from the trunk and opened the door for her.

"C'mon," he encouraged.

She glanced up, eyes wary.

He crouched beside her. "I know you're scared. But you've got to trust me." He extended his hand and waited. His leg burned fire clear down to his toes, his mind raced with images of black-hooded men wielding silencers.

He put his other hand to his wound and gritted his teeth against the pain. He knew he couldn't rush her.

She stared hard into his eyes and he struggled not to look away. He'd betrayed her once. If she spotted that in his eyes, she'd never get out of the car.

"Okay," she said, but didn't reach for his hand.

He straightened and stepped back. She shifted out of the car, swaying as she gained her footing on the damp earth. He resisted the urge to scoop her up in his arms and carry her to the bathroom. She wouldn't welcome the gesture.

Trust—he had to gain her trust.

She limped to the women's bathroom. He followed close, cursing fate for crippling her and cursing himself for letting it happen.

He picked the bathroom lock rather than ask the gas station attendant for the key. The smell of stale urine and strong disinfectant made him gag as he opened the door. She blocked the doorway and pointed to the sign that read Women.

"I'm not letting you out of my sight. Not for one minute. We can both change in here," he said.

She narrowed her eyes and planted her hands on her hips. Pretty gutsy, considering she had an assassin on her tail.

"If I was going to hurt you I would have done it by now. Trust me until I can get you safe, okay?"

He wanted to reach out, to slip the flyaway strands of auburn-streaked hair from her face.

Tentatively, she stepped into the bathroom and he followed, locking the door. He placed the bag on the sink and pulled out clothes: pants and a top for her, jeans and a T-shirt for him.

"I guessed your size." He handed her navy cotton pants, a print shirt and sneakers. "They might be a little big."

The room was too small for two people to stand in, much less change in. She eyed the clothes dangling from her fingertips.

"I'll look the other way. Pretend I'm not here," he said.

But there was no way he'd be able to pretend he was alone. Her essence still captivated him. It wasn't her scent or looks or anything he could put his finger on.

It was her.

Turning his back, he stripped the black knit top from his torso. He washed mud from his hands and glanced in the mirror. Her expression chilled his heart. Her eyes grew wide with horror as she studied his naked torso, the clothes clutched to her chest like a shield.

The scars. She was shocked by the pattern criss-crossing his back.

"Please get dressed." He didn't recognize the sound of his voice.

Ripping his gaze from her, he slipped on the T-shirt and reached for his belt. His vision started to blur.

Damn, not now. Okay, so he'd lost a fair amount of blood. He could make it for another half hour. He had to.

Stripping off his pants, he heard her gasp. She must have caught sight of the bullet wound. The lead grazed him good, leaving his thigh bloodied and raw. He grabbed the gauze and tape from the backpack and did his best to patch himself up. He managed to pull on his jeans and the room started to spin. He pressed his forehead against the dirty tile wall and struggled to breathe. The overhead fan roared like a B-52 bomber. He was going to pass out.

She touched his shoulder and he rolled his forehead against the cool tile. He could barely make out her eyes. But he remembered their color: blue like the virgin sea, clear and honest. She placed a handful of moist paper towel to his forehead. He came back a little then. The world stopped spinning quite so fast.

"Thanks."

He closed his eyes and remembered the first time he saw her, dressed in her pink lab coat. She'd been fumbling with test tubes and beakers, chewing on her lower lip in concentration and poking at her black-framed glasses with her forefinger to keep them in place.

"Your glasses," he muttered, knowing she needed them, yet also knowing he couldn't move from this spot if his life depended on it. But he wanted to get them for her. He wanted to care for her and protect her, even if she hated him for what he'd done.

He touched her hand, just as he'd touched her for the first time a year ago. He'd never forget the surprise on her face or the heat that followed. He'd never forget the passion that haunted his dreams every night since.

It was pure and right, and never before in his life had he felt this way about a woman. Never before had one touch consumed him beyond reason. And that's why he could never have her.

Her fingers trembled beneath his touch and he opened his eyes. Confusion creased her features, her eyes darkening with need, a need he remembered well.

She jerked her hand away.

"Don't...don't be afraid," he breathed heavy against the tile. He was all right when she was close, soothing him. The minute she stepped away, the world vibrated with static, his focus blown to hell.

The bathroom door squeaked open. She was going to run. Like before.

"Don't," he pleaded.

The crash of the door knifed his heart. With flattened palms, he slid down the tile wall to his knees. He'd lost her again. Lost her to fate and fear and his dishonorable nature.

What a pitiful end to it all: passed out in a gas-station bathroom, with the woman he loved out on her own, running blindly from sure death.

No. He wouldn't let her die. He pushed to his feet and stumbled across the tile floor, clinging to the wall for support. Blinking away the pain, he yanked open the door.

He squinted into the darkness, rain spitting in his face as he hovered in the threshold. A flash of movement caught his eye. She didn't stand a chance without him. She was so innocent, so helpless.

Stepping into the rain, he took a deep, fortifying breath.

"Annie!" he howled into the night. The ground started to slip out from under him. "Annie, come back!"

Chapter Three

She froze. The chill from the metal car keys raced up her arm. What had he called her?

Annie.

Her legs wobbled and she leaned into the car. Voices assailed her, one voice in particular, a woman's voice.

Annie, bring your sisters in for breakfast! Annie, make your bed! Annie, put away those critters and do your chores!

The singsong voice comforted her, yet paralyzed her with remorse. Memories flashed, sharp and quick: the scent of lilacs, sunshine warming her cheeks, sand oozing between her toes.

She whipped open the car door and crawled inside wanting to get away from Sean and the memories he'd evoked.

Annie, come home. Annie...Annie...

She shoved the key into the ignition and gripped the steering wheel. Oh God, she didn't know how to drive, did she?

Annie girl, you're smarter than anyone I know.

A sob caught in her throat. Her mother.

It's okay to be different.

She welcomed the comfort of her mother's voice, yet her insides ached as if someone had jammed a knife in her chest and twisted hard.

"Annie!"

She jumped at the sound of Sean's voice.

He pounded on the window, his face scrunched in pain. "Open the door!"

His chest heaved. "Annie, please?"

Annie. Her special name. Sean knew this name. He was her only link to her mother and at the moment, she didn't have a connection to another living soul.

She couldn't trust this man, but right now she *needed* him. Her pulse quickened and an ache started deep in her chest.

What was this man to her before she'd lost her mind? Lover or enemy? Or both?

She'd find her mom and cut this overpowering man from her life. She didn't need him. She didn't need any man.

A shaft of pain sliced through her.

"Let me in the car!" he demanded.

She didn't want to, yet had no choice. She hit the unlock button. He flung open the door, reached over her and jerked the keys from the ignition.

"Don't ever do that again, you hear me?" He

loomed in the open door, his eyes blazing fire, his teeth clenched in a near growl.

She swallowed hard.

"Do you want to die?" he said. "Do you?"

She shook her head, wondering if she should have taken her chances with the rainstorm and Zinkerman's man. Sean looked terrifying: blood smeared his hands, and rage flushed his cheeks bright red.

"Don't you know what they'll do to you if they find you?" he said.

She glanced away, remembering the aggressor who tore her from a sound sleep with brutal force.

"I don't like this any more than you do, but we're stuck with each other."

Glaring out the windshield, she interlaced her fingers in her lap. Temporary, this was only temporary. She'd remember, find her family and get away from this creep.

Her family. They were out there somewhere. Her chest ached.

"I have to get my stuff. Change into the clothes I gave you," he ordered, tossing her clothes.

Ordered. Always ordered. She blinked, and tears of frustration burned her eyes. Vulnerable and helpless. So utterly helpless. And more than a bit scared.

A few seconds passed and her skin tingled from the heat of his gaze on her body.

"Just don't…" His voice trailed off. She glanced

up, into his eyes. They'd softened to a warm green. He suddenly looked tired and beaten.

"Don't leave me," he said, his voice cracking.

He shut the door and disappeared into the bathroom. She dug her nails into the dash as adrenaline raced to every nerve ending in her body. It took great effort to control her reaction, to prevent him from seeing how much he'd affected her. Fear, anger and something else unfurled in her belly, something hot and cold at the same time.

She wished she didn't need his help. If only she could find her mother on her own.

"Why can't…I remember?" She pressed her fingertips to her temples.

Blank. Her mind held nothing but bits and pieces, images of numbers scribbled in a notebook, a large room with a high ceiling, lace-trimmed socks on her feet.

She had to move forward. She pulled off her pajama top and slipped on the print shirt, relieved it bloused in front, hiding her chilled nipples. She glanced out the window, making sure he was still inside the bathroom. She peeled the pajama bottoms from her legs and stuck her bare feet into the cotton pants. Once dressed, she tied the sneakers he'd given her, then ran her fingers through her hair, wishing she had a band to tie it back.

A minute later, he appeared with his backpack and plastic garbage bag. Sliding onto the vinyl seat, he winced and tossed the bag in the back.

"We'll get rid of this someplace else," he said. "They'll track us if they find blood-stained clothes."

Blood. That's right. His leg. He'd been shot by her attacker at Appleton. Shot trying to help her.

Don't feel sorry for him. He wants you for his own sick purpose.

Buckling her seat belt, she glanced up. He blinked slowly as if trying to clear his vision.

"Are you…okay?" she asked.

His eyes radiated a kind of emotional pain she prayed never to feel herself. It made her want to reach out, to stroke away the demons that haunted him.

No. She was mixed up, that's all. Grateful to him for saving her life. Breaking eye contact, he reached across her, his arm brushing against her thigh. Her breath caught and she closed her eyes.

He snatched a cell phone from the glove box, and pulled onto the farm road. She studied his profile, his stubbled face and hard set to his jaw. How would she convince this man to help her find her mom?

"I've got her," his said into the headset.

His rough voice shot goose bumps across her shoulders.

"Nope…yep. Not bad." She spied his hand clutching his thigh. "Someplace safe… I thought you said… What problem?" Panic edged his voice. He kept his eyes trained ahead as if he knew she was watching him. "I don't like it… I'll get back."

He slapped the phone onto the vinyl seat between

them. She could tell it took every ounce of his self-control not to scream, or worse. She sensed he wanted to hit something.

They wound their way up the rural farm road in silence. She stared out the window, trying to figure out how to get away from Sean and find her family. He wanted her to stay with him and he outweighed her by at least fifty pounds—all muscle. His white-knuckled fingers, wrapped tight around the steering wheel, made her feel slight and frail, like a delicate piece of crystal. She wondered if she'd break at his touch, shatter into a million pieces. She hugged her midsection.

"They want me to bring you in," he said.

She glanced at him.

"I work for the FBI. You might know something that could help us solve a case. Do you remember Raymond Phelps?"

She closed her eyes. Raymond. The scent of cinnamon tickled her nose. Then nothing.

"No," she said.

"You lived with him for the past fifteen years."

"My husband?"

"Your guardian."

Her guardian? But why would she need a guardian unless…no. Her throat swelled, her mind swam in images of loss. Wheat-blond hair, pale blue eyes, a comforting smile…gone.

Her mother must be dead. Why else would she

need a guardian? There was no one. No one to love her. Loneliness welled up inside. She grasped her throat, her vision blurred. Why was it so cold?

The chill of emptiness welcomed her, pulled her down, swallowing her like a pearl in quicksand.

"What the hell?" he pulled over and grabbed her shoulders forcing her to face him.

"Annie, what is it? Damn it, talk to me."

His deep voice faded. The strength of his hands warmed her tender skin. He wanted her to stay here, with him, in this place filled with evil. No reason to stay. Her mother was gone. Men wanted her dead. She didn't belong here, she'd never belonged...

"Damn it, Jackson, do it," Sean demanded into the phone. He paced the dumpy motel room. He didn't dare look at the bed.

One hour. She'd been out for sixty long minutes.

"I can't break into the Appleton system. Not using traditional methods," Jackson said. The quirky technology expert had a lot of good qualities, but breaking the rules wasn't one of them.

"Break into the system," Sean demanded.

"I'll need authorization."

"Screw authorization."

"Aren't you supposed to bring her in?"

"If you can't figure out what meds they had her on, there will be nothing left to bring in. She's unconscious, damn it."

A heavy pause filled the line. Sean needed this guy's help.

"Listen," he started, "we've got to find out what they were giving her that brought her around. I want Raymond Phelps out of circulation and this woman has the power to do it. If you can't hack into their computer system, I'm going to have to break into Appleton."

Jackson sighed. "Give me a couple of hours."

"Thirty minutes."

"Hell, I'm not that good."

"Right now, I need you to be great."

Sean hung up and took a deep breath. He'd nail Raymond Phelps if it killed him. He rubbed his thigh. The bleeding had stopped, but the grating pain still hurt like hell.

Not as bad as Raymond was going to hurt when they locked him away from his money and power. Sean couldn't believe what that guy thought he could get away with.

Annie.

Raymond practically bought her from her family, locked her up with books and chemical supplies and treated her like a lab rat. She never did see it that way. It would have taken an ounce of common sense to figure out she was being used and manipulated by Phelps. Common sense, something Annie definitely lacked.

He glanced at her slight body enveloped in shadows. The brilliance of a genius wrapped in the innocence of a child. What a combination. He knew people weren't as innocent as they looked. Hadn't he spent the past twelve years putting "innocent" people away? Criminals, all of them, abusers, like his old man.

"Son of a bitch." He paced to the window and pushed aside the worn, rust-colored curtain with his forefinger.

Stay focused. This isn't about the bastard who tried to break you.

Studying the handful of cars in the parking lot, he wished he could have taken Annie straight to the boat, but he couldn't risk it. What if she needed to be rushed to a hospital? He glanced at her still body, stretched out on the double bed. Guilt hammered away at his conscience for not getting her to a hospital.

But questions would be asked, the word would get out, and Zinkerman's men would come crashing down on them with guns loaded. Sean couldn't risk losing her to these men. She was too…valuable.

"Too valuable," he muttered, hating the sound of the words.

Nailing Phelps was the goal, nothing else mattered, and Annie was the one person who held the key.

"I don't believe you…" she whispered from the bed.

He took three cautious steps toward her as if navigating a minefield. Her head writhed from side to side and her fingers crunched the bedcovers.

"I thought…you loved me," she muttered through trembling lips. "Mom loves me. I want to go home."

Rooted in place, he watched her relive their last conversation. Did she remember what he'd done? How he'd used her to gain valuable information about Raymond?

"Raymond!" she shouted and sat up. Looking around the room, she clutched the covers to her chest.

When her gaze landed on Sean, she seemed to look right through him.

"Where am I?" she said.

"In a motel. You passed out. How do you feel?" he asked as softly as he could. Relief coursed through him.

"I'm scared. Why am I so scared?"

Without thinking, he took her hand. He couldn't help himself. "You're okay."

Her eyes widened and her gaze drifted to their hands.

"I'm sorry." He slipped his hand from hers and paced to the vinyl chair across the room. He should have known physical contact would terrify her.

"I saw this face," she whispered. "An older man…pointed chin and dark eyes."

"Raymond," he said, settling in the chair.

"My guardian?"

He nodded.

"My mother…is she…dead?"

"No, your mom's fine." He leaned forward, wanting to go to her again.

"I can't remember," she said, her voice cracking. "It's like…my head is stuffed with cotton. Why can't I remember?"

"Take it easy, honey." The endearment slipped past his defenses. "You've been through a lot—the accident, brain trauma." *Being used by people you thought loved you.*

"I don't like you," she blurted out.

He fisted his hands to calm his trembling fingers.

"You scare me," she said, a little softer this time.

He warmed at the raw honesty. The old, naive Annie was surfacing. He hoped her memory of their supposed love affair didn't surface, as well. That would throw her for a loop.

"I'm sorry if I frighten you," he said.

"It's just that…" She fingered a hole in the bed-spread. "You're so big."

That brutal honesty again. He smiled. "Don't be afraid of me." *Be scared as hell of me.*

"How do you feel?" he said. "I was worried."

"I feel goofy, like I drank a bottle of wine. Do I drink wine?"

"Once in a while." His chest ached with the memory of a lazy afternoon and a bottle of chardonnay. Damn fool.

"Do you know a lot about me?" she said.

"A few things." As much as the average husband would know about his wife.

"What's my favorite food?"

"Toss-up between mashed potatoes and licorice."

She placed her fingers to her lips and his body automatically tightened.

"I don't remember what licorice tastes like." She glanced up. "My favorite color?"

"Purple."

"Do I like chocolate?"

"Not as much as grape bubble gum."

"What's my favorite book?"

"Anne of Green Gables."

"TV show?"

"You never missed Monday night pro wrestling."

"Wrestling." Her gaze shot up to meet his. "How do you know all that?"

"I was working undercover as your bodyguard for the FBI. I was with you most of the time."

"Then why can't I remember you?"

"The accident caused serious swelling around your brain."

Because I ripped out your heart and squashed it under my boots.

"Do you remember anything at all?" he asked, hoping she'd remember where she hid evidence that could put Phelps behind bars.

"I remember the hospital. Nurse Lydia. The day you came…" She edged to the opposite side of the bed.

"Annie?"

"It was you." Her blue eyes widened.

"Annie, calm down."

She shifted off the bed and stumbled backward toward the bathroom. "Too fast in the car. You did this."

He stood, extending his hand. "Annie, wait—"

"No, I remember…you hurt me."

Backing up, she fumbled into the bathroom and locked the door. Hell, how could he blame her for wanting to get away from him? She was right. He did hurt her. Only, it wasn't the way she thought. He hadn't driven her car off a cliff. She had done that all by herself out of anger and confusion. And pain.

"Annie, unlock the door," he called through the cheap wood.

"No."

"What if you pass out like before? I'm here to take care of you."

"Go away!"

"I can't help you if you're locked in there."

"I don't need your help."

"I care about you." A knot balled in his chest.

"You're lying!"

"Let me help you."

"If you want to help, get my mom or Raymond."

"I can't do that," he said.

"Why not?"

"Come out and I'll explain."

"No!"

He went for the jugular, knowing her honor would drive her to do most anything.

"Listen to me. You were working on a scientific formula that could hurt people if it falls into the wrong hands."

"I don't believe you. I wouldn't create something bad. I'm good. I'm a good girl."

He gripped the doorknob at the sound of panic in her voice. Had he pushed her too far?

"Open the door," he demanded.

"Leave me alone!"

"Open it now or I'll break it down."

Silence.

"Annie!"

The image of her passing out and banging her head against the porcelain tub drove him nuts. He took a few steps back, and then rammed the door with his left shoulder. Once, twice. On the third try, the door popped open.

His breath caught at the sight of her curled into a ball in the bathtub, her arms wrapped around bent knees and her teeth chattering as if she'd been frozen in a block of ice.

"Don't…hurt me," she said through clicking teeth.

His blood ran cold. Memories flooded to the surface. His mother's wails, his father's grunts.

The pale yellow bathroom walls closed in, suffocating him. He took a step back, then another. Before he knew it he was in the parking lot, looking up into the rain.

He grabbed the cell phone from the rented sedan and punched in his boss's number, then ambled toward the pop machine behind the office. Too bad it didn't spit out pints of whiskey.

"Agent Connors," his boss answered.

"It's MacNeil."

"Everything under control?"

"She woke up. You talk to Jackson?" He dropped four quarters into the machine and punched the cola button for a quick sugar buzz.

"Gave him the unofficial go-ahead. Also, the psychologist says not to pressure the woman. If you force her memories, she could regress."

"What am I supposed to do?"

"Let her remember on her own."

"She remembers Raymond."

"Really?"

"Just his face." He flipped the metal tab and soda fizzed over the lip of the can.

"What else does she remember?"

"That's it." He hesitated. "Listen, I need off this one."

"Why?"

"In more than ten years, have I ever asked to be reassigned?"

"No. You burned out?"

"More or less." He placed the cold can to his forehead.

"I don't like it. The fewer people involved in this case, the better. For the woman's sake."

For Annie's sake, he needed to be as far away from her as possible. He couldn't stand her purity and innocence. He knew, if ordered, he'd chew her up and spit her out again to reach his goal. Maybe it was time for a new goal.

"MacNeil?"

"Yeah."

"Stick with her for a couple of days. I'll see what I can do."

"Sooner." He didn't know how much more of this he could take: Annie playing twenty questions one minute, being terrified of him the next.

"I'll do what I can," Connors said. "Sounds like you could use a vacation. Fly to some island and have some half-naked woman bring you umbrella drinks."

"I'll think about it."

He shut the phone and stuck it in his back pocket. A vacation is exactly what he didn't need. No, he needed to dive into a new case, chase down another bastard like Raymond Phelps and put him away for life. All a vacation would do is force him to think about things that kept him up at night.

He had to get away from Annie, her sweet voice and gentle nature—and from the gut-wrenching fear he read in her eyes when she looked at him.

Although naive, she was smart enough to be scared of him, to know what he could do to her physically and emotionally.

"It's my job," he muttered to himself, running his hand through wet hair.

His job. Get the bad guys. Put them away for life. Make sure they wouldn't hurt anyone ever again.

He'd almost nailed Phelps. The FBI was so close to exposing his plan to release a dangerous virus and then hold the world hostage by offering the only cure—Annie's vaccine.

But Raymond's order to have Annie killed threw a monkey wrench into everything. Sean would blow his cover unless he did as he was told. He had no choice: one way or another he had to purge Annie from his heart.

That's when it became clear to Sean that he and Annie could never sit on a front porch sipping lemonade, and never take a vacation in the Grand Canyon as he'd promised. It was all a game of make-believe.

Only, he couldn't help but fantasize about what a great mother she'd be. He couldn't forget the image of Annie naked in his bed, reaching out for him, opening and closing her fingers like she did when she wanted something.

And she'd wanted him. She'd made that painfully clear on more than one occasion. But he wasn't real. He was a pretend lover with a cast-iron heart and guts to match. Cold, emotionless guts coupled with an animal magnetism that had drawn her in and made her fall in love with him. Cold, heartless guts passed down from generation to generation of MacNeil men.

He stilled at the memory of her eyes just now, round with fear, her body curled into a defensive shield. To think the woman had everything taken from her in the past year: her family, her memory…love.

"No!" he pounded his fist against the soda machine.

She didn't really love him. It was a first-time crush, infatuation that lit the sparkle in her eyes whenever she'd paused from her work to smile at him. It was a sheltered girl's need for attention by someone other than a father figure.

She didn't know the real Sean MacNeil, didn't know what he was capable of. But she knew now.

Her eyes no longer sparkled when she saw him. Fear and loathing darkened the pale blue. She didn't know who she was or why people wanted her dead, and the only man who could help her was a monster without a conscience.

"A monster that scared her half to death." He cursed and started back to the room. As long as she was his assignment, he'd do right by her. He'd go back and apologize for scaring her, try and explain why he's so worried about her health.

If only he knew the answer to that himself.

On the other hand, her fear and distrust would keep things in perspective until Connors sent another man. Through her eyes, Sean would be reminded of what he really was, forcing him to forget about absolution from this woman. Her fear would keep them apart.

He approached the motel room door and knocked softly. "Annie? I'm coming in."

He slipped his key in the door and turned the lock.

Darkness clogged his vision, a shaft of light peeked out from the bathroom door.

"Annie?" He blinked to get his bearings.

He heard a squeak from the corner and the hair bristled on the back of his neck. He reached for his gun. Something whacked him in the head, sending the weapon flying and Sean to his knees. A cord snapped tight around his neck, pinching the air from his windpipe. He gasped for breath as stars danced across his vision. He could barely make out the image of Annie, tied to a chair, her body shaking.

The helpless look in her eyes shot adrenaline to every nerve ending in his body. She was going die because of his incompetence.

He edged his fingers between the cord and his neck. No good. He couldn't loosen the grip.

"No chance, man," his assailant whispered into his ear, giving the cord a quick jerk to increase the pressure. "Let's hear ya squeal. C'mon."

"Enough!" a man ordered.

The cord ripped free, slicing across Sean's skin. He gasped for air and was hit from behind, flattening him to the musty carpet.

Cold steel pressed against the back of his head. "Should I kill him?"

"Not yet," a second man said. "We need answers first."

Chapter Four

"We've been looking for you, MacNeil," a man said from the bathroom doorway. He wiped his hands on a grayed towel. "We've got a lot to talk about."

Sean was a dead man.

"The name's Hatch." The man took a few steps toward him and extended his hand. Sean glared at it.

"No? Okay, we'll get right down to it. My partner and I have been ordered to find the lady and take her someplace safe. That is, after we figure out your role in all this."

"I'm her husband," he choked out.

Hollow laughter bounced off the paneled walls. "I don't think so. But I'm curious what you want with her. She's not exactly a beauty queen." Hatch fingered Annie's hair and she whimpered, recoiling at his touch.

Sean lunged at the bastard, but Hatch's man whacked him across the shoulders, sending him facedown to the floor.

"But then her lack of beauty never stopped you from enjoying her company before," Hatch taunted.

Sean held his breath. Not like this. She couldn't find out the truth from a bastard who would twist everything, making it ugly and obscene.

"You see, Annie," Hatch continued, stroking her hair, "you fell in love with this man and he used your feelings for a little personal recreation. Isn't that right, Mr. MacNeil?"

He didn't move, couldn't breathe. She searched his eyes as if needing reassurance that he wasn't like the rest, that he hadn't used her and spit her out.

"She was a sex toy to you, nothing more," Hatch said.

"Don't," is all he could say.

"You didn't care about her, did you, MacNeil?" He nodded at the thug, who kicked Sean in the ribs for encouragement. He bit down hard to prevent any sound from escaping his mouth.

Don't give him the satisfaction. His childhood mantra for whenever Eddy came home drunk, looking for a fight.

"You never cared," Hatch said. "Admit it."

His associate delivered another kick. Sean struggled to breathe against the pain of bruised ribs.

"Say it!"

"I never cared." He glanced at Annie and her pained expression tore him apart.

But he had to buy time, had to get his advantage

back. Hell, if these jerks figured out he was FBI, they'd put a bullet in his head without a second thought. Good thing he'd left his badge in the car.

"She must be a good lay for you to risk your job as her bodyguard." Hatch touched her cheek, and she closed her eyes in disgust.

Sean's heart pounded against his chest.

"Don't worry. We'll take good care of her. We'll make sure she gets back where she belongs."

Sean leaned against the bed and glanced up into Hatch's eyes. He wouldn't be intimidated by this jerk even if the last thing he saw was the bastard's mocking grin.

"The boss doesn't know what to make of you," Hatch said. "Why would you keep her locked up in a hospital when everyone thought she was dead? I hate to imagine what you did to her, acting as her husband."

He opened and closed his fist, ready to lay one right between the jerk's eyes.

"I think it's time we found out exactly what you're after, other than Annie's virtue."

Something cracked against his skull and pain exploded behind his eyes. The room tilted sideways as he was dragged onto the bed. He blinked, trying to clear his vision, trying to shake off the static crackling in his brain.

"Just relax, Mr. MacNeil. It will be over soon." Hatch's voice grated across his nerve endings. Sean glanced at Annie, so fragile and helpless. She actually looked worried about what they were going to do to him.

They wouldn't do it in front of her, would they? Enjoy their ruthless game of torture to show her how cruel they could be?

They couldn't. Not in front of innocent Annie. He tried to sit up, but pressure against his chest pinned him to the mattress.

"Where's the needle?" Hatch said.

"I don't have it."

"Then pour this down his throat."

Someone yanked his hair, tipping his head back. He tried to pull away.

"Keep still." A hand clamped hard against his throat. Cutting off air. Cutting off thoughts. Blackness coming, pushing him down.

"Hold his nose," Hatch said.

The hand released his throat and he gasped for breath. Then something plugged his nose and liquid clogged his throat. He couldn't breathe. He started to cough. His eyes watered. A hand slammed his jaw shut and the liquid crept down the back of his throat, burning its way to his chest.

"Find out what he's after. Then kill him. We can't afford any loose ends," Hatch said. "I'll take her back."

Back? Back where? To the hospital where Zinkerman would administer mind-altering drugs to terrorize information out of her?

No. He struggled to focus. Shadows danced across

the dimly lit ceiling. Hatch…taking Annie away. His mind whirled. Losing control. He couldn't help her. He couldn't help anyone. Not Mom…not his sister, Sarah…not Annie. A failure again.

"Annie," he moaned and rolled onto his side. He had to get up, protect her.

"You're not going anywhere." Something knifed across his wrists, pinning them above his head. He couldn't move his arms. Could barely breathe. Could barely think.

"Problem?" Hatch said, sounding far away.

"He should be out by now."

"Give him more. Make it an overdose. But get what you can before he dies."

He heard Annie squeal as she was dragged away. He'd die and she'd think he was like the rest, that he'd used her for personal pleasure.

That wasn't it. There had been something more, something beyond the assignment, beyond physical attraction. Something he didn't deserve.

The door slammed shut, sending a cold shudder through his chest. They had her. His fault. Never very smart. Eddy always said so. With a strap and a growl, he'd remind Sean where he came from, what he was destined for.

Sean had nearly forgotten. He thought getting the bad guys absolved him, released him from the incredible shame.

Shame that tore apart his insides. He'd failed. Annie would pay. Only this time, with more than her heart.

ANNIE STUDIED her abductor. She focused on the man's foot pressing the pedal, and then watched his black-gloved hands hold the wheel of the car as they sailed down the farm road. She'd have to know how to do this if she was to escape.

Where would she go? Couldn't think about that. She had to get away from this monster even though he claimed he wanted to help her. She glanced at her still-bound wrists. He wanted to help her like he wanted a root canal.

She saw what he had done to Sean: bound and drugged him, left him to die.

Regret tore through her. It shouldn't. Sean was the enemy, too. Yet she saw something else in his eyes, something…

Stop thinking about him. Focus on your escape and getting to safety.

Hatch hummed a strange tune, as if he couldn't be happier. He was self-serving, like Sean who'd used her…for sexual recreation? The thought should repulse her. It didn't. She had developed an attachment to him, to a man who had used her. God, she hated that feeling.

She glanced at Hatch. He considered her a nuisance. So did Sean. So had…

Dad. She clenched her fists and fought back the wave of shame. All she wanted was for someone to…

…love her?

"You put up quite a fight back there," Hatch said. "You have to believe me. We're on the same side."

Sure, and she was the Easter Bunny.

"The man who hired me is very concerned about your health, about all those formulas you've got locked inside that pretty little head of yours."

Right. *Now* she was pretty.

Staring out the passenger window, she planned her next move. They kept her alive because of her brains. What would this monster do if she admitted she'd lost her mind?

She wasn't about to find out. She'd finally awakened to the wonder of consciousness and no one was going to take it away. If she had to lie, cheat, hurt another human being, she'd do it if it meant staying alive.

"How do you feel?" he asked with mock concern.

"I'm a little fuzzy."

"Fuzzy?"

"Confused. That man kidnapped and threatened me. He was so…so…"

Her mind filled with images of a broad-shouldered, muscular Sean whispering to her in the dark, telling her what television programs she watched, what kinds of food she ate. He knew so much about her, so many intimate things.

"Go on. He was what?" Hatch pressed.

"Mean."

He chuckled, a slight curl to his lips. "Don't worry. I'll take care of you."

She closed her eyes and pretended to be somewhere else, any place but beside this man. He had no intention of protecting her any more than Sean did. She was done relying on others. They always let her down. Somewhere, deep down, she knew this to be true.

"Where are we going?" she said.

"Appleton. There was a mix-up with Dr. Zinkerman. We've cleared it up. Everything will be fine."

Sure it will. Hatch and the doctor would exact whatever information they needed from her brain and dump her like an old sofa. Or worse, they'd send her back to la-la land, courtesy of hallucinogenic drugs. Not happening.

She stared at his right leg. Right pedal—faster. Left pedal—slower. The left foot didn't do anything.

"Annie, did Mr. MacNeil tell you why he kidnapped you?"

"No."

"Did he call anyone?"

"No." She didn't know why she lied. She didn't owe Sean anything.

"Do you remember the car accident that put you in the hospital?"

"Car accident?"

"I should probably tell you…" he shot her a sympathetic look.

She wanted to slap him.

"Not only did Sean MacNeil seduce you, but he was hired to kill you, as well."

Anger welled up inside. This man was trying to manipulate her. She could feel it. She also felt a thread of truth to his words.

What was Sean to her and why couldn't she remember? She closed her eyes and struggled with flashes of memory. An older man handing her an elegant gown, showing her how to walk, how to speak. A pair of purple lace socks…under her gown…showing them to Sean in the corner of a grand ballroom. He'd smiled at her socks, his eyes lighting up and his left cheek dimpling. Her chest warmed at the memory. His smile was a rare event.

Yet he was doing his job as an FBI agent. Gain her trust, secure her love. Why? At the motel, he'd told her he wanted information about her guardian, Raymond. Did he suspect her of wrongdoing, as well?

It didn't matter. It was time to find her family, the people who really loved her. She'd do it on her own. She'd do everything on her own from this point on. She sensed she'd let others take care of her in the past, others who didn't love her, but wanted something in return. No more.

Mom would make things right. She had to get to Mom.

"Hatch, I need to, um, go to the bathroom," she said.

"Right now?"

"Yes. I think it's the medication they had me on."

"You'll have to go in the bushes," he said with a disapproving tone.

He pulled the car to the side of the road and shoved it into Park. "Hurry up."

"Can you undo my hands?" She stretched her wrists out in front of her.

He impatiently untied the leather cord. "Make it quick."

Jumping from the car, she headed for a thick mass of trees, big trees sure to have shed massive branches. She fumbled through the brush until she was no longer visible to her abductor. Picking up a hefty branch, she crouched down and hid. She squeezed her weapon, the bark pinching the soft flesh of her fingers.

She might be confused, but she knew damn well Hatch was no ally. And neither was Sean. He admitted he'd never cared for her, that he'd used her.

Now it was her turn. She'd get away from Hatch and go back to Sean. She wouldn't save him because she cared about him. She'd make that clear. She didn't care one milligram what happened to him as long as he led her to Mom.

Weapon in hand, she struggled to calm her breathing. Sean wouldn't be leading her anywhere if she didn't get to him in time. She steadied the branch across her right shoulder, ready to swing.

A terrible thought gripped her. What if Sean was already dead? Wasn't that the plan? For the brutal man to discover his secrets, then kill him?

Panic bubbled up inside. Sean dead. It shouldn't matter. He didn't care about her, didn't love her. He had used her like all the rest. No, something was different about him. He couldn't die. Not until she found out the truth about her mother…about him.

"Hatch!" she cried to speed things up.

"Annie?" he said. "Where are you?"

The beeping of the open car door gave her hope. The keys were still in the car. All she had to do was knock him out and make a run for it. And figure out how to drive.

Yet she had bigger issues at hand. She wasn't a violent person by nature. Could she really club the guy?

"What are you doing back there?" he growled over her shoulder. She jumped to her feet and swung the branch, catching him on the side of his head.

He went down in slow motion, his eyes registering shock, then nothing. She dropped the weapon and hobbled to the car, stumbling on weakened legs.

She climbed into the car, her hands trembling as they gripped the steering wheel. The key was in the ignition, but the engine wasn't running.

"Think, think." She closed her eyes and remembered how Hatch turned on the car. She twisted the keys and put her foot on the right pedal. The engine roared and she jumped in fright. The car didn't move.

"Calm down. How did he do it?"

She took her foot off the right pedal and pulled on the metal bar until the pin read *D*. The car lurched forward and she shrieked. She slammed her foot on the left pedal.

Taking her foot off the left pedal, the car started to roll. She tapped the right pedal, getting the feel of the car's movement. She could do this.

Pressing down on the pedal, she gripped the wheel and glanced at the needle as it slowly crept to thirty. Good enough.

Sweat from her fingers made the steering wheel slippery. Would Sean still be alive when she reached the motel, conscious enough to tell her where to find Mom? What about her pursuers? Who would protect Annie from them?

"Stop thinking so much," she muttered, her eyes burning with concentration.

The rain had stopped. Thank goodness she didn't have to contend with that. But she would have to contend with a bigger threat when she got back to the motel—the man ordered to kill Sean. Cripes. She'd surely awakened without an ounce of common sense. Here she was, driving along a winding farm road with little or no driving experience, planning to save a man from a killer.

Who do you think you are? Little Orphan Annie?

She's a bookworm!
A freak!
A weakling, freakling!
Children's voices pummeled her thoughts.

"I am not a freak," she ground out.

Is that why she lived with a guardian? Because she was considered a freak by most people's standards? Her family probably sent her away because they didn't want her around.

A memory flashed: very young…asking questions in the kitchen…pineapple wallpaper. Too many questions. Driving him crazy. Driving him away—

"No!" she cried, almost missing a sharp curve in the road. She had to focus on driving and shove back the pain that welled in her chest whenever she thought about her father.

Instead, she thought about Mom and two other girls, her sisters. There was laughter, a sense of belonging.

Glancing at the speed indicator, she realized she was going thirty-seven miles an hour. She'd get there before it was too late, before Hatch's man had stripped Sean of his mind.

She sighed, grateful that she'd come out of her stupor. Things were slowly starting to surface: something about a microscope…a rabbit…getting better, hopping around in its cage.

Mending a sick animal. Always mending. Bruised ribs. Sean's ribs. Annie taping them, touching his lightly haired chest, the pads of her fingers on fire, tracing across his rib cage, fingering the hardened nipple.

"God, what did he do to me?" He really had her under his spell. How else could she explain her elevated pulse when she thought of touching his bare chest?

"Where's the motel?" she muttered, squinting into the distance.

Truth be told, she sensed she wasn't an expert navigator. She remembered something about a paper bag and getting lost. Now how was that possible? Her mind clicked off possibilities. She felt the onset of a headache.

The glow of a neon sign reflected off the wet road ahead. Slowing down, she eyed room number seven. It was dark.

Steering the car behind a secluded spot of trees, she considered her options. She might have knocked out Hatch, but she surely couldn't wrestle a six-foot male to the ground.

The motel room door opened and Hatch's partner sauntered out, a satisfied look on his face. She ducked, watching him get into a black car.

Loss coiled through her chest. He'd killed Sean. And with him went any chance of finding her mother.

The man drove off. She took a deep breath, and stepped out of the car, the crisp fall air taking her breath away.

Wrapping her arms around her midsection, she shuffled across the street to the motel. The jerk hadn't bothered to shut the door. Why should he? It wasn't as if a dead man could get up and walk away.

She stepped inside the room and closed the door. Her pulse raced. One dull light glowed by the bedside, illuminating Sean's broad shoulders as he lay on his side. She inched toward the bed and touched his shoulder. He flopped onto his back, eyes wide and lifeless. Green eyes dulled by death.

She stumbled backward into the table, knocking the lamp to the floor with a crash. Bile churned, creeping its way up her throat. She sprinted into the bathroom and emptied the contents of her stomach into the toilet.

Sean was dead. Gone. No one to help her find her mother. No one to protect her.

No one to love her.

She retched again and moaned into the porcelain bowl.

Had he loved her?

Forget about it. The bad men wouldn't give up until they found her. But that wasn't the only thing that paralyzed her.

Her hands started to shake. Sean. Sean was dead.

Dizziness pulled her down. She had to fight it off, grab hold of her senses and analyze a way out of this mess.

Standing, she ran a washcloth under cold water, squeezed it out and pressed it to her cheek.

You're one smart woman, Annie Price.

Sean's voice…echoed in her head, just before he'd kissed her. His lips, soft and full, pressed gently against hers.

She gasped at the memory, so real and intense. And now lost.

"Sean," she choked, wanting answers about who he was and what they were to each other.

"Not again," a man's voice moaned.

She clutched the washcloth between trembling fingers and stared into her reflection. She must have imagined—

"No…no more."

She raced to the bed. His eyes were glassy, perspiration beaded across his forehead. Perspiration?

"Please," he moaned.

The guttural plea crept up from his chest and touched her heart. He was still alive.

"Don't hit me." His voice cracked like that of a young boy's.

His brain was pickled in some kind of hallucinogenic drug.

Experiments. She remembered. It took time for chemicals to work their way through an organism's system. The drug could have only gone so far in fifteen or so minutes.

She grabbed him by the shoulders. "Get up!"

His head lolled to the side.

"Fight!" she demanded. "You're so damn big."

6

She pulled him into a sitting position and shook his shoulders. "I'm not done with you!"

He had to expel the drug from his system.

"Get up. Don't you give up!"

Moaning, he got to his feet. Shouldering his armpit, she led him to the bathroom.

"They've beaten you. They're winning because you don't have the guts to fight back."

She hoped her bitter words would keep him moving. If she sensed one thing about him, it was his determination to beat the enemy.

"You know what Hatch called you?" she taunted.

Only four more steps to the bathroom.

"He called you a worthless piece of trash."

"Trash... Eddy said... Don't...no more," he mumbled.

"He said you're a gutless, weak, stupid man. Is that what you are, MacNeil? Are you stupid?"

"Not stupid... I'm not stupid, Eddy." Something flashed in his eyes and she didn't care who Eddy was as long as the memories made him take one more step.

He stumbled across the threshold of the bathroom and crumpled to the faded vinyl floor. She collapsed, as well, exhausted from supporting the weight of a well-built man. She took a deep breath and closed her eyes, searching her mind for a way to purge the drug from his system.

She went to the bureau and rummaged through his bag. She fingered a travel-sized bottle of shampoo. Memories flashed across her mind. Swallowing shampoo so she could blow bubbles from her mouth. Her throat burned as the shampoo came back up. That's it, she needed to make him gag. His body would do the rest.

She went into the bathroom, knelt beside him and tipped his head back.

"Not again!" He swung his arms in self-defense and the back of his left hand smacked her in the head. Her temple stung where he'd caught her with his silver ring.

The dull throb shot anger through her, making her more determined than ever to save this man and find Mom.

Straddling him, she tipped his head back, pinched his nose and emptied the small bottle of blue liquid into his mouth. He coughed and shoved at her with more force than she thought he had left. She slid back across the vinyl floor. He gagged, lurched forward and retched into the toilet bowl. A few minutes later, he moaned.

She should go to him. Rub his back or get him a cool washcloth.

She didn't move. Touching the man was not a good idea. She needed him for information, that's all. She didn't care what happened to him after that. Why should she? He didn't care about her.

He retched again, then went still. She thought he might have passed out. Instead, he groaned and looked up at her. Confusion colored his bloodshot eyes.

"You…you came back for me."

Chapter Five

Her heart pounded against her chest as his eyes pinned her in place. It sounded as if—

He coughed again and leaned over the porcelain bowl. She sprung to her feet, anxious to get away and wipe the intensity of his words from her heart.

Closing the bathroom door, she paced to the window.

You came back for me.

His words tied her stomach in knots. He said them with such relief, such love in his eyes.

No! In his drugged state, anything he said shouldn't surprise her. He probably had her confused with an old girlfriend. She bet he'd had quite a few of those. But *Annie* wasn't one of them—not a real one, anyway. He'd used her. That was clear.

Now it was her turn. All she needed was her mother's name and phone number. Not his protection, not his help and definitely not his love.

Especially not his love.

She pushed aside the worn curtain and bit back the hollowness in her chest. She wished she could remember, clear the cobwebs and regain the ability to distinguish her friends from her enemies.

Sean clearly fit into the latter category. The last twenty-four hours proved his goal was to use her to obtain information about the man named Raymond, her guardian. That's all. Sean's interest in her was strictly professional.

Her interest, on the other hand, was personal. This was her life they were messing with: Sean, Zinkerman, Hatch and his partner.

Stay focused. Find Mom. Then she'd reconstruct her memory and move on, away from this nightmare and away from Sean.

The bathroom door squeaked open, and she turned. He leaned against the doorjamb, running a washcloth along the back of his neck. His chest heaved in and out. He tipped his head back and ran the cloth across his stubbled jaw.

Fascinated, she watched the sheer masculinity of a man who only seconds ago had been crumpled like a pile of mush on the bathroom floor.

"How do you feel?" she said to be polite. It wasn't as if she cared. She wanted him to get enough of his wits back to give her the information she needed. She crossed her arms over her chest to steel herself from her body's response to him.

"A little dizzy," he muttered.

If Sean could get to the bed and lie down for a few minutes, maybe he could get his bearings back. He took a step and his knees buckled. He started to go down but something gripped his arm, supporting him.

Annie.

She came back for him.

Every muscle in his body felt like mush as he sank into the mattress, his mind fogged from remnants of the drug. He struggled to open his eyes, his lids heavy and tight. Annie's presence filled the room. Her body set off an awareness he couldn't comprehend. She'd had that effect on him since the first day he'd seen her, peering into a microscope and tapping her foot.

"How did you get here?" he asked. "Where's Hatch?"

"He's lying in the woods up the road."

"What?" He sat up, grabbing his head to stop the spinning.

"I clubbed him," she said matter-of-factly.

"You what!"

"How else was I going to get away? Ask for the car keys?"

She stared him down, arms folded across her chest. She was different somehow. But one thing hadn't changed: she was their best lead to Raymond Phelps.

"We've gotta go," he said, planting his feet to the floor. It tilted sideways and he wasn't sure what would happen if he tried to stand.

"*We* are not going anywhere," she said.

His gaze shot up to meet her cold, defiant eyes. Yep, something had definitely changed.

"I came back for my mom's address," she said. "That's it."

Her words sliced his heart. He should have known. She didn't care about him, not after Hatch had spit out the truth.

Even if it wasn't the whole truth.

"You're not safe. I need to protect you," he said.

"Like you protected me before? By seducing me? That is what you did, isn't it?"

Her words hung in the air between them. How could he deny it?

"It's not that simple," he said.

"Did you or did you not set out to make me fall in love with you?"

"If you fell in love, that was your own fault." He stretched his neck.

"Well, that justifies it, doesn't it? What was I, some kind of idiot?"

"No."

"I get the feeling I was gullible and trusting. Am I right?"

"More or less." He rubbed the back of his neck. Damn, if the room would only stop spinning.

"And you used that trust to get close to me."

"More or less."

"Wonderful. I can hardly wait to remember the

rest." Tapping her foot, she glanced at the ceiling, then at Sean.

His heart skipped a beat. *It wasn't like that, darlin'. We had more, much more.*

"I need to find Mom," she said. "Surely you can understand that."

He looked away. He understood all right. Just not from personal experience. Hell, neither of them would have any future experiences if they didn't get out of here.

"We've got to go. Help me up." He extended his hand, not daring to look into her eyes. He couldn't stand the gleam of hatred that burned there.

"Where's my mom?" she said, refusing to help him.

"Annie, we have to get you safe. Then we'll talk about your mom."

"I'll be safe with Mom."

"Don't be a fool." He hated the sound of his voice, but couldn't control the panic that settled low in his gut. "You think she can protect you from these men?"

"That depends. I don't even know who 'these men' are."

"We don't have time for this."

"Where does my mom live? I want her phone number."

"That's the first place they'll look. Don't you get it?"

"I'm not the one who nearly died just now," she said. She was right. He had nearly died, but she had saved his life. He pushed to his feet and swayed. "We've got a problem," he said.

"Just one?"

He started for the door and grabbed his bag. With a hand on the doorknob, he paused to get his balance.

"I don't know how Hatch found us," he said. "Unless he's got someone working inside the Bureau. Which means we can't trust anyone but each other."

"You've got to be kidding."

Her cynical tone cut through him like a knife.

"Let's go." He pulled open the door.

"Not until you tell me where Mom is."

"Don't push me, Annie. I'm all you've got right now."

"That goes both ways. The way I understand it, I've got something up here—" she tapped the side of her head with her two fingers "—that you want."

"Not in your present state you don't."

"Then let me go."

"Can't do that. It's my job to protect you."

She glared at him, her eyes making it clear how she felt about needing his protection. A part of him wished he had to deal with the old Annie: naive and trusting and definitely not this damn stubborn.

"Does my mom live around here?" she pushed.

He glanced into the parking lot. She couldn't have clubbed Hatch that hard and if the jerk made his way back, they were both dead.

"Get in the damn car," he ordered.

"No."

His temper brewed. Couldn't she see he was trying to help her? No, they never did. And they always came back for more. She'd probably end up running back to Raymond and his thirty-room mansion and servants.

Over Sean's dead body. The only place Raymond was going was to prison. And if Annie didn't cooperate with the FBI, she was going with him.

"This is the last time I'm asking you to get in the car," he said, his voice more controlled than he thought possible.

"I'm not going anywhere with you."

His next move was an ugly one, but she left him no choice.

He dropped the bag and closed the distance between them, pushing aside the buzzing in his ears. He got within an inch of her, backing her against the wall. His heart skipped at the fear in her eyes, fear tempered with defiance.

"Do you really want to mess with me?" he said.

He was so close he could make out the dark ring of gray trimming her clear blue eyes. Her lips, pursed in a thin line, trembled only slightly.

"Do you know what I could do to you?" he threatened, not knowing how else to get her into the car and away from danger. "Remember how terrified you were when I broke down the bathroom door? I'll do whatever it takes to do my job. Never forget that."

Acid swirled in his gut, eating away at his stomach lining. But he knew the truth behind his threats. Although this was an act to scare her into submission, he knew a vein of violence ran deep and wide, waiting to consume him.

Her tongue danced out to wet her lower lip, and all thought exploded from his mind. Damn if he didn't want to kiss her. Her lower lip, slightly fuller than the top, beckoned to him, dared him to get a taste of its honey sweetness. A sweetness he'd sampled over and over until he'd become addicted to it. To her.

Her purity and goodness had intrigued him, then offered redemption. That's why he'd wanted to take her in his arms and bury himself deep.

He balled his right hand into a fist to ease the tension in his chest. "You're coming with me, Annie. Even if I have to carry you."

He recoiled at the sound of his false threat. He'd be lucky to walk out of here on his own two feet, much less carry a hundred-plus-pound woman over his shoulder.

She glared at him, and for a minute he thought she might call his bluff. His shoulders ached with anticipation.

Then she shoved her upturned palm at his chest.

"Keys," she demanded.

"What?"

"You're in no condition to drive."

"Are you kidding? You don't drive."

"How do you think I got here? Flew on my magic carpet?"

"I didn't think—"

"No, you were too busy trying to get your senses back. Give me the keys."

He slipped them from his pocket, still trying to process the fact that she'd driven Hatch's car. She'd always been chauffeured before, treated like royalty.

Swiping the keys, she marched past him and made her way to the car as if his physical threat had no effect on her whatsoever.

He noticed the determined set to her jaw as she slid behind the wheel of his rental car. That was one thing that hadn't changed. It took amazing determination and great patience to develop the formulas she had created.

Sliding into the car, he wondered if patience was the weapon she planned to use on him. Wear him down until he finally spilled the whereabouts of her mother. He'd have to be careful with this Annie. Although her brilliance had temporarily escaped her, she'd gained a savvy Sean hadn't seen coming until it had smacked him head-on.

She shoved the key into the ignition, then glanced at him.

"I need something from you," she said, her eyes pleading.

God, if only that were true.

"What do you need?" he said, his voice raw.

"Tell me something about Mom. Give me something to hold on to."

"I can't."

"I have nothing. No one."

She placed her hand to his shoulder, and he clenched his jaw. His resolve started to unravel.

"I need to know she's out there," she said. "Give me something. A time zone? A country?"

He felt a tug on his heart. She hadn't forgotten how to do that.

"Listen, you said we have to trust each other," she said. "Tell me something about her. Help me trust you."

Big mistake, lady. Don't ever trust me.

"Sean?"

"Vermont. Your mom's farm is in Vermont."

She cracked a smile and he realized he hadn't seen that warm-hearted grin in a very long time. He missed it. He missed her.

"Thanks," she said. "Once we're safe, you'll take me to her, right?"

"Sure," he lied. What choice did he have? He needed to keep her close. Needed her to trust him. Somehow, he'd make her understand that visiting her mother wasn't wise.

"It's a deal, then." She reached out to shake his hand. He thought it an odd gesture, but one consistent with the old, naive Annie.

He wrapped his fingers around her hand and the heat from her skin set off a slow burn in his chest.

She tugged her hand free and cleared her throat as if she, too, felt something beyond that of a gentlemen's agreement.

"Where to?" she said.

"That way," he pointed.

She shoved the car in Reverse and hit the gas. It jerked backward, nearly slamming into a spruce tree.

She hit the brakes and shrugged. "First time using the backward."

"Reverse."

"Whatever. Where are we going?"

"Someplace where no one can find us."

Turning the wheel, she crept onto the farm road. At this speed, they'd make it to the boat by Christmas.

She clutched the steering wheel and accelerated to a whopping thirty-four miles per hour. The feel of a slow ride soothed his nerves. His eyelids drooped. No. He had to stay awake. Everyone was a potential enemy now. Even Annie.

He blinked and looked at her. "I don't suppose you remember anything?"

"Doesn't sound like there's much worth remembering."

His heart sank. She knew she'd been used. That's what she had accused him of doing on that cold February night just before she drove herself off a cliff. Used by the one man she thought loved her. Was it any wonder she refused to remember?

But he had to jar something loose. They had to find the formula before it, and the dangerous virus, fell into the wrong hands. Before *she* fell into the wrong hands.

"You were helping with an FBI investigation before the accident," he prompted.

"Tell me more about the accident. Maybe that will help."

He sucked in a breath. "It was dark, you were driving on a winding road. Visibility was low."

"But you said I don't drive."

"You didn't." He looked away. The old Annie was brilliant but naive. He could manage that, manipulate her emotions and sometimes even her thoughts. Yet somehow she'd awakened with a sort of instinct that she'd never had before.

"Why was I driving?" she asked.

"You were upset. You took off in one of Raymond's cars."

He curled his fingers around the door handle. He couldn't tell her the whole story. She'd die without his help, and if he blurted out the truth, she'd run again.

"What was I upset about?" she said.

"I'd rather you remember on your own."

They drove fifteen minutes in silence. He struggled to stay awake, to fight the drug's relaxing effects.

"Tell me if I've got this right: Raymond is my guardian. He hired you to protect me. But really you're an FBI agent who seduced me?"

He nodded.

"Boy, what you guys will do for your country."

He cleared his throat.

"Or was the seduction part your idea?"

He stared out the window. "I had a job to do."

"Which was?"

"Find out everything I could about the formula you were working on."

"Did you get everything you needed?"

The double meaning of her words tore him apart. He got more than he deserved, something so close to love it scared him senseless.

"Not everything," he said.

"Then you're not done with me."

Her tone shamed him, shined a light on the dishonorable methods by which he'd gained her trust.

Taking a deep breath, he stared her down. "The formula you were working on would neutralize a dangerous Level Four virus. If one person gets control of it, he would be very powerful," he said.

"I can barely remember my name, much less some magic formula."

"Your memory will come back in time," he said, dreading the moment she remembered the things he'd said to her that fateful night.

"I remember some things in flashes. Dr. Zinkerman gave me exercises to do at the hospital to help me remember." She sighed. "I still can't believe he's one of the bad guys."

"You know things that could greatly affect many people. You can't trust anyone."

"Not even you?"

What could he say? She couldn't trust him. Not really.

"Right now, I'm all you've got," he said.

"Oh, that's comforting," she muttered.

He glanced out the passenger window. He couldn't pass this case off to anyone else now, not with the possibility of Zinkerman having someone on the inside.

Zinkerman, the mystery doctor who miraculously had brought Annie back to life. Damn, Sean had forgotten about the drug.

"How are you feeling?" he asked.

"You mean other than not knowing who I am, having been kidnapped and accosted twice in one night?"

"I'm serious. Are you dizzy? When was the last time you had your medication?"

"Last night."

"How often did they give it to you?"

"Once a day, I think."

"Do you have any idea what it was?"

"No."

"Think!"

"I don't know," she said, an aggravated edge to her voice. "It was a little yellow pill."

"Was there a bottle? Did you see the bottle?"

"They don't exactly leave your prescription on the nightstand."

"This is serious. You passed out before. Do you remember that?"

"Yeah. I'm not that out of it."

"You passed out because you're off your meds."

"I passed out because I thought Mom was dead."

"What?"

"You said some guy named Raymond was my guardian. Why would I need a guardian unless Mom was dead? I thought I was alone. Empty inside, like before…" her voice trailed off and her fingers clutched the steering wheel tighter.

"What is it?" he said.

"Nothing…something…I don't know," she whispered.

"Annie, you've got to believe I'm going to keep you safe."

"I know that, Sean."

He warmed inside at the use of his name.

"After all, it's your job," she said.

He tried to read her expression. She stared blankly at the road ahead.

"Your job," she repeated, her eyes squinting as if she replayed a scene in her head.

"Annie?"

The car slowed to a near crawl of fifteen miles per hour.

"Annie, what's wrong?"

"Your job. Hired to take care of me…everyone hired…no one really cares…everyone pretends… they don't care…"

"Annie, that's not true."

"I remember now. You called me naive."

"Don't—"

"You said you could never really care…" her voice trailed off.

She pulled to the shoulder and jerked the car to a stop. Shoving it in Park, she glared at him. "Get out."

"What?"

"Out!" she shouted. "I'll find Mom. I don't need you."

"I'm not going anywhere."

"Fine."

She whipped open her door and took off into the forest.

"Damn." He got out and started after her, his leg throbbing, his head spinning. "Annie! Get back here."

"Go to hell!" she called over her shoulder.

Anger drove her deeper into the forest. Annie had a feeling she'd never forget Sean MacNeil, the pain, the betrayal. It still only came in bits and pieces, but a very big piece had slapped her upside the head— Sean didn't care about her. He didn't love her.

But she had loved him. He'd made her feel whole and alive.

Yet it was all make-believe to get what he wanted.

She eyed a thick mass of low-hanging spruce, hoping to lose herself in the needled camouflage. One thing for sure, there was no way she'd stick with Sean MacNeil. No way in hell.

She was done with being used, especially by people who were supposed to love her. Her heart pounded in her chest. Who else pretended to love her? Not Mom. She knew Mom loved her with all her heart. But then why did she send Annie to live with Raymond? So many questions.

"Annie!" he called.

She pushed through the mass of green as fast as her bruised body could manage. Running off into the wild wasn't one of her more brilliant ideas, but her heart was calling the shots, driving her farther into the forest, away from the man she'd originally coined the devil.

And that's before she knew anything about him.

Her foot caught on a fallen tree limb and she stumbled, swinging her arms to get her balance. She fell on a patch of green ivy, cool and damp against her cheek. Every muscle in her body ached, but she wouldn't give up. She took a few deep breaths and pushed up to her knees.

The determined grip of Sean's hands pulled her to her feet. She didn't want this man touching her and hurting her again.

"Get away from me." She blindly swung at him.

"What's the matter with you? Didn't you hear a

word I said? They'll kill you." His green eyes radiated anger.

Rationally, she should be scared of him and what he could do to her. But she was too upset to be rational. She was too hurt.

"Let me go," she struggled to free herself. "I know how you feel about me. You think I'm stupid, you think—"

His mouth came down on hers, absorbing the sound of her accusations. Firm yet soft, his lips demanded a response. Incredible warmth filled her chest. She'd been cold for so long. But now, now she felt safe and loved.

By the devil?

She started to push against his chest, but he pulled her closer and deepened the kiss. A moan bubbled up from deep inside her, escaping her throat in a rumble that seemed to ignite his desire even more. With one arm wrapped around her waist, the other buried in her hair, he pulled her against him as if he couldn't get enough. She couldn't fight this. Not when her body ached for something so bad she thought she'd explode.

A memory flashed to the surface: Annie digging her nails into the bronzed skin of his back, crying out, flying high above the clouds. Heat pooled between her legs, her nipples grew hard. She wanted him to touch her there, to drive her to the edge and bring her back again. She knew he could do it. He'd done it before.

And it felt so right.

She gripped his shoulders and tried wrapping herself around his body. His moan vibrated against her lips, a mating sound that shot deep to her core. Her fingers clenched the hard muscles of his shoulders as she tried to get closer, still closer.

He broke the kiss, his breath hot against her cheek.

Her mind swam in confusion and her body trembled with unfulfilled need. He was the enemy, yet she wanted him inside of her.

Tipping her head back, she studied his dark green eyes. The anger that sent her racing into the woods was a mild emotion compared to what she read in his eyes: layers of raw pain that made her own chest ache.

There was more to this man than the images of her scattered memory. Much more.

"I'm…I'm sorry," he said, glancing down, struggling for breath.

"Now *that,* I remember," she said.

Chapter Six

"You remember? What do you remember?" Sean said, staring intently into her eyes.

"Kissing. Your lips. The taste." Oh boy, the taste.

"What else?"

"Nothing."

"What did you remember in the car?"

She glanced at the blue sedan. Something had upset her terribly, a flash of…Sean's horrible words.

Words he didn't really mean, did he? There was such pain in the memory, yet such truth to his kiss.

"What's real?" she said, her gaze drifting to meet his eyes.

"Death," he said. "That's very real. And it's right behind us."

With a gentle tug of his hand, he led her through the brush and back to the car. She studied their entwined hands. His grip wasn't demanding or hurtful. On the contrary, he held her fingers gently, as if she were a fragile creature lost in the midst of chaos.

Well, that about described it. Chaos is what whirled in her brain, thrilling her one minute, shaming her the next. She wanted Sean, yet he was the enemy, at least she thought he was the enemy. She wasn't entirely sure what to make of this man.

"Next time, don't run," he said as they approached the car.

"But—"

"Listen." He turned and took both her hands in his. "I know it's scary, not knowing who you are or who you can trust. But you've got to believe that whatever I've done in the past, I'm here to help you now, okay?"

She believed him. In a place deep inside that had nothing to do with common sense or intelligence.

He squeezed her hand. "I'll drive."

"Are you sure?"

He nodded.

She slid across the seat, her heart still racing.

"We need to find out about your medication," he said, getting behind the wheel. "That's probably contributing to your mental state."

"My mental state?"

"Yeah. You're a bit…unbalanced. You were never like that before." He punched a number on his cell phone, then pulled onto the road.

A horrible thought taunted her. What if he didn't feel the sparks when they kissed? What if it was all strategy to get her to trust him and help him solve his case?

"What if I never remember?" she asked.

"You will, eventually."

"But if I don't—"

"Jackson, it's MacNeil," Sean said into the phone. "No, I had to move… Yeah…why not?"

He spoke confidently to his associate, as if nothing were wrong, as if his world hadn't been rocked by the kiss he'd shared with Annie.

If only she could say the same. Her skin tingled and she still tasted him on her lips.

She needed to remember and find Mom. Then she could distance herself from Sean and get a hold of her perspective. Annie and Sean: something didn't fit. She was an intellectual and Sean, although not stupid, seemed driven by physical intimidation and violence. What drew them together?

Then again, if she was naive and he had street smarts, he could easily manipulate her feelings for his own purpose. He'd made it clear he'd get the job done at any cost. But what would it cost her to trust this man with her life?

She leaned against the headrest and let out a sigh. A few hours of sleep would be nice, not to mention a cheeseburger. Her stomach growled.

"You okay?" he said.

She assumed he was speaking to his associate.

"Annie!"

Her eyes shot open and she glared at him. "What?"

"I asked if you were okay?"

"I thought you were still on the phone."

"I hung up. How are you feeling?"

"I could use a cheeseburger," she blurted out.

He cracked a smile.

"What's so funny?" she said.

"A cheeseburger?"

"Yeah, why?"

"You weren't a big junk food fan before."

"What was I into?"

"Your research, mostly."

"All the time?"

"That stuff takes time, Annie. You developed a treatment for a rare genetic disease called FD that affects children. You also worked on vaccines for a few other viruses. I don't know all the details."

"Did I have a social life or friends?" she said.

"Not really. When you weren't in the lab, you read a lot and wrote in your journal. When you did break for meals, you'd have the cook make meat loaf or chicken and dumplings."

"I sound boring."

"You were never boring." He stared straight ahead.

Silence filled the car like helium in a balloon. The man was so controlled, so cool. Which made her wonder if the kiss was a ploy to get her back in the car.

"Annie, we might have to go back to Appleton."

She sat straight, panic ringing in her ears. "But they'll find me...Dr. Zinkerman will be there. They'll drug me again and…and you said you'd protect me." She reached for the door handle.

He grabbed her left arm and pulled her against his chest. He wrapped his right arm snugly around her shoulder, making it impossible for her to fling open the door.

"See, it's that kind of thing that makes me think you need your meds. What were you going to do? Jump out of a moving car?"

"I can't go back there," she growled into his chest, her fingers scrunching the soft cotton of his shirt.

"Just listen, okay? I need to get your medication. My guy hasn't been able to break into the hospital computer, so we have no idea what you were on. I don't want you to lapse back into a catatonic state. Can you understand that? I can't lose you like that again."

She closed her eyes, reveling in his words. He cleared his throat and she scolded herself. He was worried about losing her precious mind, not the woman he held in his arms.

He loosened his hold, but she didn't make a move to push away. She needed comfort from his hard body. For a second, she let herself believe this man could protect her from anything, even her own memories.

"I'll break into Appleton," he said.

She opened her eyes and studied his angular jaw clenched tight. "It's really that important that I regain my memory?"

"You have no idea."

Her heart sank. Her memory. Formulas and research and who knows what. He didn't care what it would do to her to remember the past. Her personal well-being was probably the least important thing on his list.

She scooted to the other side of the car and stared out the window, wishing she could pretend none of this had happened, that she was someone else, someone he loved for herself, not for her smarts. A familiar sadness washed over her.

Her stomach growled again.

"We'd better get you some food and find a place to bed down for the night," he said.

"I want to go home," she said, scratching her arm.

"Home?" He narrowed his eyes.

"I need to see Mom."

"Oh."

She sensed his relief. What did he think she meant?

"Darn mosquitoes," she muttered, the itching creeping up her arms to her neck.

"Annie?"

"What?" She scratched her cheek.

"Your face, it's all red."

She flipped down the visor mirror. Her heart leaped into her throat at the sight of red blotches covering her cheeks. She studied her hands and arms. The same reddish pattern crept up to her elbow.

"Oh, my God! What's happening?"

SEAN WAS LUCKY as hell that Spencer's Truck Stop had a vacancy, and even luckier that the store carried antihistamines. He'd secured a room and dropped off Annie, then hid the car behind a barn up the road.

He needed to stabilize her condition, which meant getting Annie to trust him enough to take the damned antihistamines. His medical expert at work said knowing what he did of her medical history at Appleton, the over-the-counter meds should be safe.

"I don't need a bath." She clutched a pillow to her chest and curled up in a ball on the motel bed.

"It's poison ivy," he said. "It's not dangerous, but it can be miserable."

"How would you know? You're not the one who's got it."

"I stepped in it when I was a kid. Not fun."

"You're making that up," she challenged, sounding like a child.

"Nope. I was eleven years old." He walked to her side of the bed and sat next to her.

"And your mom put you in the tub?"

"Yep," he lied. His mom was too scared of Eddy to give her son the attention he deserved. Sean's neighbor, Mrs. Casper, was the one who had brought over the oatmeal bath and pink lotion.

"Why is it getting worse?" She ran her hands up and down the sides of her arms.

"Because you're itching."

"It hurts."

"I know. Here, drink this." He held out a plastic capful of liquid antihistamine.

"What is it?"

"Something to stop the itch." And hopefully calm her down.

She sniffed it, then itched her elbow.

"It's grape-flavored," he urged. "C'mon. Swallow it and you'll feel better."

He had to stop the reaction before it became serious, possibly affecting her breathing.

She downed the capful of liquid, made a face and grabbed the glass of water sitting on the nightstand. She took three swallows.

"Okay, bath first, then lotion." He pulled her to her feet.

"I can bathe myself."

"I can't risk you passing out on me. Especially after taking the antihistamine. It makes some people loopy." He grabbed the box of anti-itch bath salts and made for the bathroom.

"I don't need an audience," she protested, following him.

"I won't look."

"Sure you won't."

He couldn't help but smile. She'd developed a sense of humor during her long sleep.

He closed the lid of the toilet seat. "Sit."

She did, crossing her arms over her chest.

He ran the bath water and poured anti-itch granules into the tub. "You'll feel better after this."

Out of the corner of his eye, he caught sight of her scratching her face.

"Don't." He grabbed her wrist. "You're only making it worse."

"I can't help it."

"Think about something else."

"That's a joke, right?"

"No. C'mon. Think about something to keep your mind off the itch."

"The brain's empty, remember?"

"Close your eyes."

"Why?" Skepticism laced her voice.

"Just do it."

She closed her eyes and stuck her chin out as if to warn him not to mess with her.

"Picture yourself on the ocean," he said.

"Am I in a boat?"

"Why?"

"'Cause I can't swim."

"How do you know that?"

"I just do."

Now he was getting somewhere. She was right. She couldn't swim.

"You're on a yacht, actually. Sunbathing."

She opened one eye. "In a one-piece suit."

"Fine, in a one-piece suit. The sun is warm. The waves rock you to sleep. Back and forth. Your mind floats along, not really thinking, just floating. Back and forth."

She opened her eyes. "Stop."

"Why?"

"I'm getting seasick."

"It's probably the medicine."

"I hate this," she muttered.

"What?"

"Being loopy."

"Don't worry, I'm here."

"Very comforting."

He ignored her sarcasm and reached for her blouse.

"What are you doing?" She batted his hand away.

"Helping you undress."

"I can undress myself, thank you."

"Annie—"

"Out." She pointed at the door.

He didn't have the heart to remind her he'd seen it all: the curves and valleys, the rosy nipples and birthmark on her right hip.

"Okay. I'll be out here if you need me," he said.

"I won't." She shoved him out the door.

"Leave the door open."

"Fine." She cracked it and he sat on the edge of the bed.

He hated not being with her, not knowing if she wobbled as she undressed. But he had to respect her privacy. He owed her that much.

"What happens after you get my medication?" she called through the partially open door.

"That depends. It would help if you could remember things, like where you hid your research."

"I hid it? Why would I do that?"

"We're not sure. Only you know that." But he suspected she'd accidentally discovered Raymond's plan to unleash the virus, and then make billions off the only known vaccine.

"Annie? You okay?" he called.

"Fine."

Humming echoed from the bathroom, an old habit of hers when she concentrated. He wondered which article of clothing she peeled away from her body. Damn, he had to stop wanting this woman. He shouldn't have kissed her. What was he thinking?

He wasn't thinking. Something else had taken over, overriding his judgment and sense of decency. After all, it wasn't decent of him to kiss her like that, even in the name of strategy. He'd promised himself that this time he wouldn't compromise what little integrity he had by manipulating her feelings.

He had to stop thinking about the woman in the next room, who was, most likely, naked, and focus on strategy for breaking into Appleton.

He heard the scrape of plastic rings across the metal shower bar, then a splash.

"How's it going?" he asked.

"I still itch."

"Give it a few minutes."

She splashed some more. "Does my mom love me?"

His breath caught.

"Come again?"

"Does my mom love me?"

A flash of Annie with her mom made him smile. He'd taken her to visit her mom and two sisters last fall. She'd left her family to study at Raymond's estate more than fifteen years ago. She had to miss their warmth. The kind of warmth that was foreign to Sean, yet something he craved.

"She loves you," he said.

"Then why was I living with this Raymond guy?"

"He discovered you."

"You make it sound like he found me in a petri dish."

Truth was, Raymond Phelps had taken advantage of both Mrs. Price's grim financial situation and her trusting nature. Margaret Price and her three girls were on the verge of being homeless thanks to her husband abandoning the family. Then in walked Raymond, their savior. He offered to pay off the farm and fund Annie's education. Her mom wanted what was best for Annie, and knew she'd never realize her potential in the small farm town. It seemed like a miracle to Mrs. Price, who'd been completely taken in by Raymond's generosity.

Yeah, what a guy.

"He noticed you at a science fair," Sean said. "He was intrigued by your intelligence."

"A genius that falls into poison ivy. Great," she said. "How old was I?"

"Seven. You went to live with him when you were eight."

"Didn't my family miss me?"

"They did, but you visited," Sean said. But not nearly enough. No, Raymond wanted to keep a tight leash on his protégé.

"Seven. I…I don't remember…being seven—" she slurred.

He stood. "Annie?"

He pushed open the bathroom door and gently slid the curtain aside. She wore a washcloth on her head and across her chest. Her fingers were inter-laced and stretched out in front of her.

The antihistamine definitely made her loopy. "C'mon, Annie. You need to soak the inflamed areas."

Kneeling beside the tub, he wondered if he could do this without losing his mind. He removed the washcloth from her head, dipped it into the water and pressed it against her cheek. He struggled not to let his gaze drift to the curve of her breast. The wash-cloth didn't cover it all. Damn.

"Keep your hands in the water, honey, so the medicine soaks them."

"I can't feel my skin. I'm sleepy." She slid into the water.

"Whoa, there." He gripped her by her arms and guided her back up. "Don't sink on me."

She leaned against the back of the tub and closed her eyes.

He splashed water across her nose. The antihistamine was doing a number on her.

"You'll have to take off your clothes," she said.

"Excuse me?"

"You can't come in the tub and play if you got clothes on. Your mama will be sooo mad."

"More likely Dad," he muttered.

"Mmm. Dad. I hate Daddy." She opened her eyes and squinted at Sean. "You know why?"

"No, why?" He ran the cloth down her cheek.

"Because he hates me. Always hate first, then you won't get hurt."

She closed her eyes.

"I'm sure he doesn't hate you."

No one could hate you.

"He does. 'You ask too many questions.' 'You never listen,'" she mocked in a deep voice. "He hated me so much he ran away."

You got off easy.

"Shhh. Annie, just relax." And keep remembering. Maybe this was the beginning. If she remembered her father, she could remember the rest of it: Raymond, the formula, the recording she'd made by accident— the reason Raymond had ordered her death. He feared she knew too much and would ruin his plans.

If only she'd gotten wise about Sean.

"What else do you remember?" he asked.

"Nothing…too sleepy."

"A couple of more minutes in the tub, okay?"

"Hmm."

He continued soaking the washcloth and squeezing it over her reddened skin. Good thing the inflammation didn't go anywhere near her breasts. At least he could keep his focus away from the parts of her body that threatened to tear apart his restraint.

"Wanna go home…" she mumbled, turning her cheek into the washcloth.

It was bad enough that she hadn't a clue who she was or who she could trust, but now her body was being attacked, as well.

"Sleepy…" she muttered.

She started to slide down into the tub.

"Whoa, there. C'mon, let's get you to bed." He snapped the towel from the bar and laid it over his shoulder. "C'mon, Annie. Work with me."

He coaxed her toward him. Her wet skin warmed his chest. He pulled her to her feet and wrapped the towel around her backside. She rested her cheek against his shirt and wrapped her arms around his waist.

"Sleepy," she whispered.

"It's okay. It's bedtime."

He dried her off the best he could and scooped her into his arms. His chest ached with memories. God, it had been so long since he'd held her like this. She buried her lips against his neck and twined her hands tightly around his shoulders. Her warmth taunted him, reminding him of the passion they'd shared.

But he couldn't be intimate with her again, even if she begged and pleaded. He knew that with Annie, it wasn't about sex; it was about love.

Too bad she didn't know Sean was incapable of loving anything but his job.

Sucking in a sharp breath, he peeled her away from his body and slipped an undershirt over her head. He knew the only way he wouldn't lose the battle of wanting to touch her was to cover the beauty that tempted him.

"Cold, so cold," she said, gripping his arms as he slid the shirt down below her waist. It just about covered everything. Just about.

His cell phone went off. He laid her beneath the covers and grabbed his phone.

"MacNeil."

"It's Jackson."

"Tell me you identified her meds."

"Sorry."

Damn, he wanted good news. He needed this case to be over. "What then?"

"Someone is trying to sell the antivirus."

"What the hell? They can't sell something they don't have."

Silence filled the line. Unless…he glanced at Annie. Had she completely finished the antivirus? Was that what she'd planned to tell him the night of her accident? She'd said when her current project was finished, she'd take him on a romantic trip for two. Before she could share her news, he'd stopped her with the truth: he was FBI, out to nail her benefactor, a benefactor who had ordered her death because she knew too much about his plans.

"Are you sure the sale is for real?" he asked Jackson.

"Ninety percent. Intercepted a few anonymous e-mails. Someone's selling something."

"You can intercept private e-mails, but you can't get the girl's medication?"

"Sorry. Hospitals."

"We really need her to remember." He pinched the bridge of his nose.

"Where are you?"

"Safe, for now. I need you to book us a flight from Boston to Miami, midday tomorrow."

"Why Miami?"

"Just do it," he ordered in the hopes of throwing their pursuers off track.

He clicked off his phone. Damn, more complications. Phelps couldn't have the formula. If he did, he wouldn't be selling it off. He'd want to keep the power of disease and death to himself.

"I'm scared," she whispered in her sleep. "Why did he lie?"

Great. Was she remembering the night Sean slashed her heart open? Bastard. Worse, he was a coward. He'd dropped the bomb and turned his back on her, afraid to see her reaction: the shock and hatred in her eyes.

He deserved her hatred. He knew that.

He just didn't know if he could survive it…again.

Get a grip, man. This is about bigger things than your pride.

"Cold. Still cold," she whispered.

He placed his hand to her forehead and she pulled it against her chest until he was practically on top of her.

"Annie, you need to sleep." He tried to pull away.

"Warm." Her fingers locked around his neck pulling him close.

Hell, it wouldn't hurt to get a few hours sleep so he'd be fresh for his second Appleton break-in.

The box spring groaned as he shifted onto the bed. She curled up against him, her fingers clinging to his shirt. He automatically stroked her damp hair, guilt beating him for the times he'd stroked her in more intimate places, all in the name of justice.

Justice. Absent so many times when he was growing up. But he'd make sure others wouldn't suffer at the absence of justice. He'd done pretty well, beating every enemy he had set out to conquer. And he'd managed it without losing too much of his personal honor.

Until Annie.

His honor had flown out the window when he'd used her feelings to get at Raymond. Where was the honor in that?

It wasn't the first time he'd felt the old man's blood pumping through his veins. Whenever Sean would go after a child abuser or rapist, he'd feel the burn start low in his gut and swell until he thought he'd burst. That's why he'd never be gifted with love or family—he couldn't trust himself to control his violent streak.

The truth was, he'd inherited a legacy of violence and manipulation from his father, a man who abused and hurt the people he supposedly loved.

For a while, Sean accepted the old man's excuses and offered pity that a normal twelve-year-old boy shouldn't have to feel for his father.

But he got wise with age. When he challenged the old man's abuse, Eddy said he respected his son's strength of character. "Take your best shot," Eddy would say. "Go on. Put some meat behind that smart mouth of yours."

Sean gritted his teeth and kept his temper in check for a while. But Eddy kept taunting him, calling him names, calling his mother names. Said she was a whore who'd slept with a garbage collector to get pregnant with Sean. And Sean lost it.

The harder he hit, the more weapons Eddy would pull from his arsenal: a belt, baseball bat, broken glass.

That wasn't justice, and it surely wasn't love. He

didn't know what love was, but knew he'd never be gifted with it himself. He was okay with that.

Until Annie. His chest tightened.

"Me…just for me," she whispered. "Only wants research."

She jackknifed and clutched the sheets to her chest. Her breath caught on a sob.

"Annie?"

She jerked around, as if surprised to find him there. Even then, her eyes didn't fully focus. Her lower lip trembled. His heart broke in two.

"No one loves me," she said.

"Shhh. It's okay. C'mon, lay down." He patted at his chest.

"Why can't anyone say it?"

In her eyes, he saw a hurt child, recognized the pain much like that of a teenage boy who didn't understand what he had done to deserve punishment instead of love. No one gave him what he needed most, what Annie pleaded for. But Sean could give it to her.

"I love you, Annie," he said, not recognizing the sound of his ragged voice.

She blinked, then settled against him, one arm tucked under her body, the other stretched out across his chest.

"Annie?"

Her fingers twitched, as if she'd fallen into a deep

sleep, content and at peace. Then again, maybe she'd been asleep the whole time.

He couldn't help but wonder if it had been justice to say the words to her?

Chapter Seven

"I have no choice, Annie." Sean slipped on the black windbreaker. He had to go back to Appleton and get her meds. She had to remember.

"But I'm better. I don't need my medicine."

He glanced at her, still bundled in the double bed. Patches of bright red splotched her pale cheeks. She looked tired, beaten and very vulnerable.

"Jackson can't access your files. I've got to go back."

She sat up. "Then I'm coming."

"No, you're not. You'll be a distraction."

She pulled the covers over her head.

"There's coffee and doughnuts on the table," he said. "I'll be back by lunchtime."

"I can't believe you're abandoning me." She ripped the sheet from her head.

Her words pained him more than she could know. He doubted he could ever abandon Annie, not emotionally, anyway.

"You'll be fine." He slid a strand of copper-streaked hair behind her ear. "Did you sleep okay?"

"I don't remember." She looked up at him and cracked a smile.

He smiled, too; he couldn't help it. Even with her life falling apart, she'd found a shred of humor to give her strength.

"You will remember, Annie. You have to. That's why I need to get the medication."

She pulled the covers back over her head. "Bring me back two hot dogs with everything."

"I'll try." He longed to pull down the covers and let her know she'd be okay, that he'd take care of her.

But it was better this way. If he gazed too long into her blue eyes, he'd be drawn in again, losing his perspective, his edge.

He reached for the door, glancing out the window into the parking lot.

"Sean?"

"Yeah?" His eyes narrowed. Something wasn't right out there. He couldn't put his finger on it.

Suddenly the image of Annie tied to a chair, trembling from head to toe, haunted him. It was just yesterday, because he'd left her alone for five minutes.

"I'd feel safer with you," she said.

Hell, if she only knew what her words were doing to his insides.

"Are you sure I can't come with?" she said.

He turned and her eyes caught his heart. He was

lost. She could have anything she wanted: his heart, his soul. He'd give it freely. Damn, these emotions were dangerous as hell. He had to keep a clear head if he was to break into the hospital and get her meds. The only way to keep a clear head was to keep her where he knew she'd be safe.

"You're coming with me," he said. "But you'll stay in the car."

She nodded and tore off the covers. She slipped on loose-fitting pants and eyed him. "Turn around."

If she only knew he'd seen it all last night. He continued to study the parking lot. He was being paranoid. No one knew where they were.

"Maybe we can find a diner on the way there," she said.

"Grab a doughnut for the road."

"Kill joy," she muttered. "Okay, I'm ready."

"You sure you're up to this?" he asked, glancing over his shoulder. She'd slipped on one of his T-shirts.

"I'm fine."

He locked the door. "We've got a little hike to get to the car."

"I said I'm fine."

He led her across a field, staying close to trees for camouflage. His leg wound seemed to be healing on its own, thank God. He didn't need an infection to complicate matters.

It felt different being with Annie today. Something had changed. She'd started to trust him, maybe.

Either that or she remembered his accidental confession last night.

I love you, Annie.

God, he hoped not. For her sake.

Within minutes they were at the car, heading toward Appleton. Time for new wheels, he thought. He'd left an old beater truck up north by the rented cabin as plan B. He hoped they made it that far without being discovered by their enemies.

Annie sat quietly beside him. He wished they were at a safe house instead of running from thugs. Damn, he wanted her safe. He needed to put this case to bed.

Bed. The very place he'd awakened this morning with Annie sprawled across his body, rubbing her cheek against his chest, moaning and making those little squeaking noises that drove him insane.

He'd never seen a more content woman, and he hadn't even made love to her. Good thing. That would have screwed him up. Saying the words had been bad enough. Words she didn't remember. Another lucky break. He didn't want her confused this time as to who he was or what he'd do to her in the line of duty.

He focused on strategy for penetrating Appleton. Having studied every nuance of the place, he knew the food service truck made its morning delivery at six. He'd sneak in with the delivery, swipe her files and hopefully some meds, and no one would be the wiser. It was a dangerous assignment for one man, but he wasn't sure who he could trust at the Bureau anymore.

For now, he and Annie had each other. He never thought he'd say those words again, not after what he'd done to her. What would she do when she found out the truth?

It didn't matter. It wasn't as if their relationship had a life of its own. It existed for one purpose only: to rid this Earth of another evil.

At least something positive had grown from Sean's violent heritage. It drove him to serve justice. During his years hunting down monsters, he'd been able to control his primal urge to beat a suspect to a pulp. He feared that it was only a matter of time before he'd lose control completely. You can't change genes. He *was* his old man.

He would have given anything to change himself for Annie.

Impossible. So, he'd keep his last shred of integrity by not hurting her again. He'd never forget the emptiness he'd read in her eyes just before she'd taken off and driven off a cliff.

Pain knifed his gut. The wreckage, steel crumpled and twisted around her small body like tentacles of an octopus. He didn't remember driving from the mansion to the wreckage, but when he got there and ripped open the door, his body started to shake at the sight of her: blood splattered across her face, her chest, trailing all the way down to her fingertips; her head tipped to the side as if it had been yanked off.

At that moment, Eddy's voice taunted him:

"You're bad like me, kid. Blood and pain. That's all you've got to offer."

"You okay?" Annie said.

Her voice shocked him back to the present. "Yeah, fine."

He would never allow the promise of love and happiness to draw him in, not when he knew it didn't exist…for Sean.

He pulled the car onto a dirt road.

"Where are we?" she asked.

"Appleton is over that ridge. I'm hiding the car so you'll be safe."

He half expected her to argue and demand she tag along.

"How long will it take?" she asked.

Camouflaging the car behind a cluster of spruce, he shoved it into Park. "Twenty, maybe thirty minutes."

She nodded and he sensed her fear.

"Annie, it has to be this way. You need your meds. No one's looking for you here. You'll be safe, okay?"

Leaning forward, she hugged him. "Thanks for taking care of me last night."

Her fingers clung to his jacket.

"Don't worry. I'll be back. Promise." That was one promise he would keep, because he had a job to do.

She released him, slipped her hair behind her ear and smiled. "I'll be here."

His heart pounded against his chest. She was so

sweet and innocent. So trusting. Damn, she shouldn't trust him.

Flinging open the door, he made his trek through the woods, desperate to get the drugs that would help her remember. She had to remember, for the safety of others, but also so she'd stop looking at him like her boyfriend and start glaring at him like her enemy.

He made his way to Appleton's service entrance and glanced at his watch. Five-fifty. The truck would pull up in ten minutes. He crouched low against a tree and waited. This was the worst part. Waiting for action. Keeping a lid on the adrenaline. Keeping a lid on his emotions.

That had been a challenge last night, especially when Annie pleaded to hear the words.

I love you, Annie.

When she woke up with no memory of the confession, relief vied with disappointment. Why? It wasn't as if the words were true. Sean MacNeil hadn't a clue what love was. The only "love" he'd known was warped with violence and pain.

Maybe that's why he could say the words so easily, as if ordering a pizza. Who was he kidding? Saying them last night had ripped him apart inside. Probably because of the lost expression in her eyes. That had to be it.

The food truck groaned up the drive and slowed at the gate. He slipped out from behind cover and grabbed the bar on the back. He rode the truck to the service entrance and hopped off aiming for the back stairs. Five minutes, tops, and he'd be in the administrator's office.

Crack of dawn was shift change, and an ideal time to break in. He climbed the stairs and opened the door to the second floor. Peering down the empty hallway, he took a deep breath, then strode to the office, picked the lock and let himself inside. He got to work at the computer, anxious for information about Annie's medical condition.

Annie. She'd been easy prey before. So trusting of Sean. He hated himself for what he did to her.

He brought up her records and scanned the documents, looking for a clue as to what mystery drug had brought her around. Maybe the lab at the Bureau could intensify the effects and bring her memory back quicker. That would solve everything. That would give Annie her life back.

And his life? Would it ever be the same after this case was over? *Forget about it.* His only concern had to be helping her remember where she'd hidden her completed research and what she'd stumbled upon that had made the old man order her death.

Sean hoped he got the chance to explain himself before she discovered from someone else what a bastard he was.

"I'd like to hear that explanation myself," he muttered, tapping his finger on the desk.

"Come on, come on."

The printer finally shot out the last few pages, including a copy of her MRI report. He grabbed the paperwork, shut down the computer and made for the door. Next stop, the hospital pharmacy. He needed to get her medication. Cracking open the door, he eyed the hallway. Empty. He bolted for the stairs, whipped open the door and he found himself staring at the badge of an almost seven-foot guard.

"And where do you think you're going?"

ANNIE HAD BEEN sitting here a lot longer than twenty minutes. Something was wrong.

She crouched behind a tree near hospital property, a shudder racing from her neck to her ankles and back up again. The sight of her former prison didn't do much for her mental state, as Sean called it. She still couldn't believe she'd been brave enough to hike across the field after him. Brave or stupid? She wasn't sure. Sometimes she wondered if Sean was right—if she'd lost her mind and needed drugs to get her wits back.

What she needed were her medical files that hopefully listed her mother's address and phone number. Her goal: find Mom. Going after Sean had nothing to do with the possibility that he'd been caught and detained by Zinkerman's men.

She shook off the memory of Sean lying on the bed in the first motel room, his eyes wide and his body listless. Hatch. Zinkerman. So many enemies.

So many bad men after her. She still wasn't sure where Sean fit into all this.

Taking a deep breath, she said a few Hail Mary's for luck. Well, that was one good thing she remembered. She rubbed her hands together in nervous energy as she waited. Nurse Lydia usually worked the day shift. She had to help.

Or would she turn Annie over to Zinkerman? No, there was a streak of compassion running through Nurse Lydia. She would listen to Annie's story first. She just hoped the nurse would believe her crazy tale. Sometimes Annie had a hard time believing it herself.

The vintage pink Cadillac slowed at the hospital entrance and turned into the drive. Nurse Lydia had told Annie about the inherited car—her pride and joy. The pink car paused at the gate. Annie ran up to it and tapped on the passenger window.

Lydia jerked in surprise and lowered the window. "Mary?"

"I need your help," she said, trying to keep her voice from trembling. The last thing she needed was to sound like a hysterical escapee.

"Get in the back and stay down," Lydia said.

A sob of relief caught in Annie's throat as she did as ordered. God, she hoped she was right about this. She hoped Lydia wasn't one of them.

"We've been ordered to subdue you," Lydia said over her shoulder. "Dr. Zinkerman claims you attacked him."

An Important Message from the Editors

Dear Reader,

If you'd enjoy reading romance novels with larger print that's easier on your eyes, let us send you TWO FREE HARLEQUIN INTRIGUE® NOVELS in our NEW LARGER PRINT EDITION. These books are complete and unabridged, but the type is set about 20% bigger to make it easier to read. Look inside for an actual-size sample.

By the way, you'll also get a surprise gift with your two free books!

Pam Powers

84

THE RIGHT WOMAN

she'd thought she was fine. It took Daniel's words and Brooke's question to make her realize she was far from a full recovery.

She'd made a start with her sister's help and she intended to go forward now. Sarah felt as if she'd been living in a darkened room and some- one had suddenly opened a door, letting in the fresh air and sunshine. She could feel its warmth slowly seeping into the coldest part of her. The feeling was liberating. She realized it was only a small step and she had a long way to go, but she was ready to face life again with Serena and her family behind her.

All too soon, they were saying goodbye and Sarah experienced a moment of sadness for all the years she and Serena had missed. But they had each other now and that's what

She held easy on that's what

Printed in the U.S.A.
Publisher acknowledges the copyright holder of the excerpt from this individual work as follows:
THE RIGHT WOMAN Copyright © 2004 by Linda Warren. All rights reserved.
® and ™ are trademarks owned and used by the trademark owner and/or its licensee.

YOURS FREE!
*You'll get a great mystery gift with
your two free larger print books!*

GET TWO FREE LARGER PRINT BOOKS!

YES! Please send me two free Harlequin Intrigue® romantic suspense novels in the larger print edition, and my free mystery gift, too. I understand that I am under no obligation to purchase anything, as explained on the back of this insert.

PLACE
FREE GIFTS
SEAL
HERE

199 HDL EE56   399 HDL EE3K

FIRST NAME	LAST NAME

ADDRESS

APT.#	CITY

STATE/PROV.	ZIP/POSTAL CODE

**Are you a current Harlequin Intrigue® subscriber and want
to receive the larger print edition?**
Call 1-800-221-5011 today!

▼ **DETACH AND MAIL CARD TODAY!** ▼

(H-ILPI-09/06) © 2004 Harlequin Enterprises Ltd.

The Harlequin Reader Service™ — Here's How It Works:

Accepting your 2 free Harlequin Intrigue® larger print books and gift places you under no obligation to buy anything. You may keep the books and gift and return the shipping statement marked "cancel." If you do not cancel, about a month later we'll send you 6 additional Harlequin Intrigue larger print books and bill you just $4.49 each in the U.S., or $5.24 each in Canada, plus 25¢ shipping & handling per book and applicable taxes if any.* That's the complete price and — compared to cover prices of $5.25 each in the U.S. and $6.25 each in Canada — it's quite a bargain! You may cancel at any time, but if you choose to continue, every month we'll send you 6 more books, which you may either purchase at the discount price or return to us and cancel your subscription.

*Terms and prices subject to change without notice. Sales tax applicable in N.Y. Canadian residents will be charged applicable provincial taxes and GST.

If offer card is missing write to: Harlequin Reader Service, 3010 Walden Ave., P.O. Box 1867, Buffalo, NY 14240-1867

BUSINESS REPLY MAIL
FIRST-CLASS MAIL   PERMIT NO. 717-003   BUFFALO, NY

POSTAGE WILL BE PAID BY ADDRESSEE

HARLEQUIN READER SERVICE
3010 WALDEN AVE
PO BOX 1867
BUFFALO NY 14240-9952

NO POSTAGE
NECESSARY
IF MAILED
IN THE
UNITED STATES

Annie closed her eyes. It was over.

"But I don't like Zinkerman," Lydia continued. "I don't know why, but after you disappeared some men came to Appleton and went through your things. They gave me the creeps. Zinkerman said they were private investigators hired to find you. Instinct told me something wasn't right. I overheard Zinkerman on the phone, screaming at someone."

Lydia sighed. "I don't know who you are, Mary, but I'd like to help."

"My name is Annie."

"Annie?"

"It's complicated. The FBI hid me at Appleton under a false name to protect me."

"And Dr. Zinkerman?"

"He's not one of the good guys."

They pulled into the back parking lot and Annie glanced out the front window at the ominous brick building.

"Why did you come back?" Lydia said, turning off the car.

"There are bad men after me because of scientific formulas locked in my brain. But my memory is sketchy so the FBI wants me to stay on the medication Zinkerman prescribed. Sean broke into the hospital to get information about the drug. I haven't heard from him in hours."

"Sean, your husband?"

Annie hesitated. "Yes."

"That's not good."

"Why?"

"Zinkerman gave orders to detain him, too. Something about your husband being involved in the attack."

She gritted her teeth. Zinkerman knew damn well Sean had nothing to do with the attack, that it was Annie, all by herself, who had rendered the good doctor helpless.

"Let's go in and find your husband," Lydia said.

Annie glanced at the building and swallowed hard.

"Annie, you know I'd never hurt you," the nurse said.

The words. Annie had heard them before from someone else. They were empty words. But right now she had to believe them.

Lydia led her into the employee lounge, where she opened a six-foot locker.

"Here, looks like you're cold." Lydia handed her an oversize sweater. "I'll go poke around. Stay put, okay?"

Annie clung to the sweater, the familiar scent of antiseptic and sickness weakening her knees. Lydia closed the door and alarm coursed through her body. Could she trust the woman? What choice did she have? She couldn't go roaming around the building by herself. Someone would be sure to recognize her and pull out the restraints.

She ran her fingers through her hair and paced the small lounge. It seemed like hours before the door opened. It was another nurse. Annie held her breath.

"Hi. Who are you?"

"My cousin, Susan," Lydia said walking up behind her. "She's checking out places for her mom who was in a bad accident."

Susan? Lord, if Annie had to answer to one more name she'd have to be put on an antipsychotic drug.

Annie smiled at the other nurse, who shrugged and ambled toward her locker.

"Come on, Susan. I can show you around before my shift starts." Lydia cupped Annie's elbow and steered her into the hallway.

"Remember the cameras," Lydia said. "Keep your head down, but act normal."

Normal? She hadn't a clue what the word meant.

"Zinkerman's not here, which is good," Lydia said. "Your husband is downstairs with security, which isn't good. They found him with your medical files. The administrator called Dr. Zinkerman."

Annie stumbled at the sound of the doctor's name.

"Smile and keep walking," Lydia whispered. "The administrator, Bill Cousins, is still trying to piece together what happened last night. There's a rumor that your husband didn't want you to remember certain things about him, he was an abuser or something."

"Bull," she let slip.

Lydia's eyes grew wide. "You remember?"

"He'd never hurt me. Not like that." She stared straight ahead.

"There's also a rumor your husband was involved in your accident."

There was some truth to those words. She knew it in her heart.

"And here's the craft room," Lydia said in her cheery voice as if giving her the complete tour of the facility.

"Sean saved me from Zinkerman's man who shot at me," she whispered.

Nurse Lydia squeezed Annie's arm. "If I take you to your husband, Cousins might detain you until Zinkerman gets here."

A chill rippled across her shoulders. She wanted to run, but she wasn't a quitter. "I need medication to last me a few weeks," she said.

Lydia glanced down the hall. "I can get it. What about your husband?"

"He committed me in the first place, right?"

"Yes."

"Then he can sign for my official release."

"But Zinkerman—"

"As long as Zinkerman isn't here he has no power. This Cousins, have I ever met him?"

"No. He has little or nothing to do with patients."

"Tell me about him."

Lydia rattled off highlights of the administrator's life: an easy job making six figures plus benefits, bi-weekly golf games and a current lawsuit filed by a former patient for negligence.

"Does he follow procedure?" Annie asked.

"To the letter."

Scenarios clicked off in her brain—theories, equations, actions and reactions. She imagined, envisioned, saw the answer in her mind's eye.

"Take me to Sean," she said.

She hadn't a clue where she got the mental fortitude to follow through with this. This entire plan could backfire, landing her right back where she started: at the gates of hell.

As they descended the stairs into the dungeon called Security, she swallowed her trepidation, step by step.

Lydia paused at the door. "I'll be back as soon as I get the medication."

Annie nodded and opened the door. Sean glanced up from his position in a chair, his wrists cuffed behind his back.

"What the hell are you doing here?" he said.

"Sweetheart!" She raced to him, wrapped her arms around his neck and laid a kiss on him to stop him cold. He resisted at first, then she felt his surrender. He leaned into her, the warmth of the kiss spreading throughout her body. She broke the kiss and smiled.

"I've missed you," she said.

"Have you lost your—"

She kissed him again, telling herself it was all part of the act. Her body argued otherwise. She loved the feel of his lips on hers, his male scent permeating her flushed cheeks. She loved the feel of hard muscle between her fingers as she gripped his upper arms.

"Excuse me, ma'am? How did you get in here?" a voice said from the door.

She broke the kiss and whispered in Sean's ear. "Trust me." His lips were still slightly parted; his eyes a combination of anger and need.

Taking a deep breath, she turned to address a giant security guard who stood in the doorway. A rotund, balding man stood beside him.

"Who are you?" he said walking toward her.

"Who are you?" she countered, her hand still possessively on Sean's shoulder.

"Bill Cousins, chief administrator of this facility."

"I'm Mary MacNeil, former patient."

Cousins's eyes widened. She tamped down her panic. She could do this.

"Why do you have handcuffs on my husband? He came for my medical records. I don't understand why he's being detained."

"With all due respect, Mrs. MacNeil, he broke into my computer for your medical records and you've not been formally released. You attacked one of our doctors yesterday."

"If my husband broke into your computer, it's because he doesn't trust you to do your job. Why should he? I've been accosted numerous times by Dr. Zinkerman. I was only trying to defend myself last night."

Annie's cheeks reddened at her lie about Zinkerman's abuse, but she needed to lie to push Cousins further into a corner.

"You're delusional," Cousins said.

"I've never been more sane in my life. Please release my husband."

"I should clear this with Dr. Zinkerman."

"Who's in charge, you or Zinkerman?"

"Well, I am, but—"

"Where's the phone?"

"What?"

"The telephone. I need to call my attorney."

Cousins hesitated.

"Then again maybe I'll go to the police, then the press. Wouldn't *Newsweek* be interested in the abuses at your facility?" She crossed her arms in a position of power.

"Uncuff him," Cousins ordered the guard.

Five minutes later Sean was officially signing Annie out of Appleton. Nurse Lydia gave Annie a hug. "I'm putting some medication in your pocket," she whispered into her ear. "Here's something else. A blank journal for you to write your thoughts."

Lydia took a step back and smiled. Something ached inside Annie's chest. A connection with another person, a person she could trust. It reminded her of a connection with someone else, someone who cared about *her,* not her brains or her research.

It had been a stressful hour, gathering all her mental and physical strength to get back into

Appleton, then bluffing Cousins into letting them go without waiting for permission from Zinkerman. Thank God the bad doctor hadn't returned.

The gates opened and Annie and Sean strolled away from the Appleton property, hand in hand. Once out of sight of the hospital guard, he slipped his hand from hers and picked up the pace.

He didn't seem happy to see her, or relieved, or even grateful. Fine. She eyed the medical file in his hand. That's all she needed anyway.

Still, his attitude irked her.

"Your welcome," she said.

He stared straight ahead, completely ignoring her.

"Great weather we're having," she said, glancing up at the clear blue sky.

Nothing.

"I could really go for a Hawaiian-style pizza."

He stopped short and stared at her. "What the hell is the matter with you? How could you walk in there like that? What if Zinkerman got his hands on you?"

"A simple thank-you would be nice."

"For what? Risking danger for your own selfish needs? This is about more than some juvenile crush you have on a man you hardly know."

A juvenile crush? Her blood pressure spiked as she watched him storm toward the car. She wanted to set him straight, to tell him the rescue had nothing to do with him and everything to do with tracking down the whereabouts of her mom. She wanted her freedom, to find the people who loved her. That's why she'd gone after him. But he hadn't given her a chance to clarify her position. He got into the car and slammed the door, slapping her medical file between the seats.

She pulled open the door and got in, ready for a fight.

"Zinkerman was on his way. Did you know that?" he said.

"Then it's a good thing I came when I did."

"Now everyone knows where you are. You might as well have shot up a flare. At least if I'd gotten in and out, they wouldn't have discovered our whereabouts."

"But you couldn't get out, remember?" She countered.

"I was working on it."

"Handcuffed to a chair?"

"Damn it, if Zinkerman had—"

"He didn't."

"They could have—"

"They didn't."

"I can't protect you if you keep doing stuff like that," he said, slamming his fists against the steering wheel.

"I'm a big girl. I can take care of myself."

Sean grabbed her by the shoulders preparing to let her have it, but the lecture wouldn't come. As he stared into her eyes, he knew what blasted his control to smithereens: she could have been hurt.

"I'm glad…you're okay," is all he could get out, then pulled her to his chest. She came willingly and a ball formed in his throat. How could something so impossible feel so right? They would have sat there for hours had his common sense not kicked in. They had to get out of here and quick.

"We've gotta go," he said against her silken hair.

She pushed away from him and smiled. "Thanks."

"For what?"

"For caring."

Clearing his throat, he started the car.

"Lydia gave me some medication," she said, glancing out the window.

He pulled onto the farm road leading away from Appleton. "Good. I'll send it to the lab for analysis. Maybe they can intensify the dosage to help you remember more. Where did you get the sweater?"

"I stole it off a patient."

His head snapped around.

"Kidding," she said, her hand up in a defensive gesture.

He headed north, toward relative safety. Annie grabbed the file and leafed through it.

"You sure you're up to that?" he said.

"It's my medical file."

A file he'd practically memorized: head trauma, broken hip and arm, internal bleeding. It was a miracle she'd survived. She flipped over another page and turned white.

He glanced at the marriage certificate. Damn.

"What's this?" she said.

"I had to prove you were my wife in order to admit you to Appleton."

"This is a marriage license, a real one? We're…married?"

Chapter Eight

Sean focused on the road, steeling himself against her horrified expression.

"But you said you weren't my husband." She stuffed papers back into the folder.

"We never exchanged vows."

"What *did* we do?"

"Nothing."

"You married me against my will?"

"You were unconscious and in danger. We had to protect you."

"I don't understand. What about Raymond? Wasn't he my guardian?"

"He thought you were dead."

He needed to keep her calm and relaxed, not upset her further with the betrayal of her father figure.

"We can't get into this right now," he said. "Not with Zinkerman on our trail. Which reminds me, what did he do to you back at Appleton?"

"Nothing, I made it up. Don't change the subject." She squared off at him. "You and I were legally married while I was in a coma?"

"Yes."

"You thought I was going to die, didn't you?"

"No."

"What if I'd remained in a coma indefinitely?"

He couldn't answer. The thought of never hearing the sound of her laughter had eaten away at his insides for the past year.

"What if you fell in love and wanted to marry someone else?" she said.

"That would never happen."

"Because you were committed to your job and a pretend marriage?"

He stared her down. "Because I don't do love. Never have. Never will."

"People don't 'do' love. It happens all by itself."

"It doesn't happen to me."

His words fell heavy between them. They had to be said. Sean had started in this world without love, and he'd go out the same way. Hell, he knew he'd been a mistake, a plan of his mother's to keep Eddy in line. She'd admitted it to him once, confessed her hopes that having a child would change her husband.

They drove in silence, Annie scribbling in her journal.

"Did you remember something?" he said.

"Nothing important." She didn't look at him.

"Everything is important. Your mind is what will free you in the end."

"Then I'm in big trouble."

"Annie—"

"Don't, okay? Don't be nice to me. Don't talk to me like you care. Stop with the lies. For once I'd like to feel clean, like I wasn't covered in a film of deceit. I get it now. I understand your role in all this. The less we talk, the better."

He wanted to argue with her, convince her that he did care about her and they could be friends. Friends? Who was he kidding? He had to keep this professional. He simply couldn't risk getting pulled in again.

He grabbed his cell phone and punched his supervisor's number, then glanced at Annie. "Can I see the medication?"

She dug out the bottle from her sweater pocket and handed it to him. Their fingers touched. A surge of electricity shot across his nerve endings. Her eyes flared. She felt it, too.

"Connors," his supervisor said.

"It's MacNeil. Tell Jackson to stop his probe of the Appleton computer."

"Why's that?"

"We went back and got her medical files, and the medication."

"We?"

"I went back. She followed."

"Judas priest, man! She's a federal witness. You shouldn't be—"

"We also got her medication." He spelled out the prescription.

"Bring her in. That's an order."

"Can't."

"Why not?" Connors pushed.

"I think they've got someone on the inside. They found us too easily last night."

"You're being paranoid. You've got your orders. Bring her in."

"I need to be sure."

"You've always been a loyal agent, MacNeil. Don't start thinking now. We'll expect you by night-fall tomorrow."

"Yes, sir."

He clicked the phone off and slapped it against the dash.

"Bad news?" she asked.

"No. Yes. I don't know." He took a deep breath and glanced at her. "You need to remember."

She looked away.

"I know a hypnotherapist we could try," he said.

"No mind control stuff."

"It's hypnosis. It will help you remember. You want to remember, don't you?"

"I'm not sure," she said through clenched teeth.

"Your power lies in your memory. They can't hurt

you if you remember and go public with what you know. You'll be safe. You can get your life back."

"My life." She touched her hand to her forehead. "I've had flashes of what I think is my life. Flashes of frustration and loneliness. Then I see your face."

She glanced at him, and the emotion in her eyes made him snap his gaze back to the road.

"If I remember, I'll remember it all, right?" she said.

"That's the idea."

"How painful is this going to be?"

He clenched his jaw.

"Thought so." She hesitated. "What happens after I remember?"

"You'll get your life back."

"From what I can tell, I was shipped out to live with a stranger because I'm smart. I spent most of my days alone in a laboratory because I'm smart. I'm on the run for my life because I'm smart. If I remember it all, I'm right back to my pathetic existence."

"Don't you dare feel sorry for yourself. You have more than…"

"Than what?"

"Forget it."

"No, I want to hear this. A lecture from the king of honor and integrity. From the man who prostituted himself to manipulate me. A man who married an unconscious woman against her will. Let's hear it. Come on."

"This isn't the time."

"Sure it is," she challenged.

"Drop it, Annie."

"Hey, you were the one who said honesty is the best policy. You want me to tell you everything. That goes both ways. What do I have? Huh? Come on."

He snapped. "You had it easy, okay? You had everything you wanted whenever you wanted it. Raymond made sure of that."

"Yeah, well, that's not how I remember it."

"You said you don't remember."

"I remember feelings." She waved her hand. "Forget it, you wouldn't understand."

But he did. That was the problem. Only he never realized that the secluded lifestyle bothered her. She'd seemed content in her lab doing research, having Raymond's servants and butlers wait on her from sunrise until dusk. She'd never told him of her loneliness.

But then he didn't listen very closely to her words for fear the naive scientist would get under his skin. So he half listened to her hopes and dreams. Trying to compartmentalize the place in his heart that was being slowly warmed by her constant wonder. It was all a lie anyway. Nothing he did or said held any truth.

Or did it?

She had professed her love for him. But he never had said the words back. He remembered the first time she shared her secret, her voice pitched higher than usual, dancing with excitement. He'd taken her to a carnival and afterward they went exploring in a forest nearby. The stars glittered in the dark sky, and the wind was crisp with the smell of the mountains.

Suddenly it hit him. He knew from limited psych training that smells can bring back memories. It was worth a shot. A five-minute stop in the forest was a risk worth taking to bring back her memory.

She'd called it an enchanted forest. That was an understatement. He'd never forget the evening spent in each other's arms.

He glanced at her. She stared out the passenger window, angry as hell that she was legally tied to him.

To think that a year ago she said she'd have given anything to marry him. She didn't really know him. He only let her see the smooth and caring facade that was nothing like the real man. Nothing like the violent animal chomping at the bit to get out and ravage the world around him.

Including Annie. He could never hurt her. Not physically, anyway. But emotionally? He couldn't risk it—didn't trust himself.

"I've got an idea to help you remember," he said, needing her to remember, needing her to hate him.

"No hypnosis," she said, crossing her arms over her chest.

"I want to take you to a special place."

"Back to Raymond?"

He gripped the steering wheel at the sound of hope in her voice.

"No, to a spot I think might jog your memory."

"Are you sure Raymond can't help? I get this feeling he always took care of me."

He opened and closed his fingers around the steering wheel. Oh, the old man took care of her all right. Right to her grave.

"We can't involve anyone else, Annie."

"So, you won't let me call Mom? Just to hear her voice?"

"I'm sure her line's tapped and they're probably watching the farm."

"She's in danger?" she said, panicked.

"They have no reason to hurt her. They're watching her to catch you."

He hoped he was right. He couldn't bear the thought of anything happening to Annie's mom. He'd met her once. His heart ached for a connection with someone nurturing and generous.

Hell. He had to get his emotional armor back in place before he completely lost his edge against their pursuers.

"Are we going back to the motel?" she asked.

"Too dangerous."

A forlorn expression creased her features. Familiarity of any kind must seem like nirvana. They'd become familiar in sleep last night even if she didn't remember. Her rounded curves fit so perfectly against him, her warmth seeping through his shirt and into his chest.

He admitted to himself that last night was the first time he'd slept in months, which wasn't a good thing. Drawing comfort from Annie made Sean weak and unsuspecting.

He couldn't afford to be either.

SHE MUST HAVE fallen asleep. When Annie opened her eyes, the sun burned low against the horizon. She glanced out the window at a corner grocery as they passed through another small farm town.

Adjusting herself into a better position, she tried making sense of it all: Sean was her husband and up until yesterday she'd been a patient at a mental hospital. Which meant he had complete control. Control that Annie wanted back.

It was time to break free of Sean and his lies, of the constant fear, of the haunting feeling that in the end she'd have no one. A part of her feared she was meant to be alone. At least that's what she'd been told over and over again.

People don't understand you.

No one appreciates your brilliant mind.

You're not like a normal girl.

She'd give anything to be a normal young woman. Then she wouldn't be running from bad men who wanted to probe her mind and kill Sean.

She studied his stubbled chin and firm set of his jaw. Determination emanated from his body. He was determined to make her remember and yet she got the feeling he dreaded it. What compelled him to be her sole protector when he could turn her over to the FBI and rid himself of the personal danger that nipped at their heels?

"Why are you doing this?" she asked.

"I think it will help you remember."

"I mean why did you marry me to keep me safe? Why did you risk your life by breaking into Appleton? Why protect me by yourself when you could take me in?"

"Which question do you want me to answer first?"

Was that humor in his voice?

"Take your pick," she said.

"We forged the marriage certificate so I could prove I was your husband and admit you to Appleton. The Bureau thought if the men wanting your formula found out you were alive, they'd track you down. We're doing this all to protect you, Annie."

"And get information from me."

He didn't answer.

"Why you?" she said. "Why don't you take me in and be done with it?"

"I don't know who to trust. My gut tells me Zinkerman or Hatch bought an agent on the inside. I can't ignore the possibility."

And I can't ignore you, Annie thought.

But she wanted to. She wished she could look at the broad-shouldered man without tasting him on her lips, without feeling the rock-solid muscle of his chest warm her fingertips.

Bare skin. Hot. Soft. His.

She rolled down her window. The early-evening wind slapped her cheeks, a slapping she deserved right now.

Sean said he didn't know who to trust. Well, that made two of them. One thing was certain—she couldn't trust her body, not when it cried out in need whenever he came within four feet of her.

Think about something else. Find a way out. You're a smart girl.

If she were so smart, why had she fallen for Sean?

Deep down, she knew she'd been in love with him. Knew he'd cast a spell on her that even the most brilliant scientist couldn't create an antidote for. He had some kind of emotional control over her, and it was time she snapped the connection. She'd never find Mom and re-create her life if her heart was held captive by this manipulative man. He expected her to share her flashes of memory, but he never shared anything about himself. It was as if he didn't really exist, as if he were a robot programmed to do his job.

She resented the fact that his job included keeping her under his sexual power. It had to be sexual. It wasn't as if she genuinely cared for such a controlling man.

A controlling man. A flash of memory tickled her thoughts, then popped into a million pieces.

"You okay?"

"Fine." She'd do anything for her freedom. But where would she go? She'd hoped to find information about her mother in the medical files. Instead, she found herself shackled to a man who continued to use her.

An hour later, he pulled onto the side of the road. "We're here. You called this your enchanted forest."

"Enchanted," she said.

He got out of the car. She couldn't take her eyes off the trees—tall, full, swaying with life. Her door opened and Sean extended his hand. She couldn't bring herself to touch him.

"Thanks, I can manage." She swung her legs out, her feet hitting the gravel with a crunch.

He pulled his hand away and shoved it into his jeans pocket as if it had been sliced with a knife. No, no compassion today, Annie thought. She had to think about herself and finding her freedom.

"We came here before?" she said.

"On the way home from the carnival at the shore. You were fascinated by the fall colors. You made me stop. You got out of the car and took off."

She approached a sign that indicated the beginning of a trail.

"Did we do a lot of things together?" She started up the path.

"I was your bodyguard. I was with you all the time." He walked within arm's reach, kicking at the leaves that littered the path.

"All the time?" She turned and quirked a brow.

"Most of the time. When you weren't sleeping."

"What else did we do?" she asked, tentatively strolling into the forest.

"Whatever you wanted. I took you to the library a lot. That place drove me nuts," he muttered.

"Why's that?"

"Too quiet."

"It's quiet out here."

"Not the same kind of quiet. Out here, you know you're alone except for nature."

"Nature and an FBI agent," she shot back.

"Don't think of me as an agent. Think of me as…" he hesitated, then glanced at her, his eyes a warm shade of green. "As a friend, I guess."

"Not my husband?"

He cleared his throat and walked a few steps ahead of her. "Stay behind me. You can never be too careful."

"Of what?"

"Animals. We don't want to spook them. That's why the rangers don't like people walking off trail."

"Don't tell me you were a park ranger in your previous career?"

"A ranger told us about spooking the animals when he kicked us out the last time we were here."

"Why? Did we scare Smokey?"

"Something like that."

He picked up his pace and she wondered what, exactly, had got them kicked out of a public park.

"You feel anything?" he asked from a good five feet away.

"Besides hungry?" She put her hand to her stomach. The doughnuts at breakfast didn't go a long way.

"You have a one-track mind."

"I can't help it. I think better on a full stomach."

He stopped dead in his tracks and stared her down.

"What?" she said.

"Nothing," he said.

She paused at a seasoned oak and noticed a heart carved into the bark. "Look." She ran her fingers over the artistic expression.

He took a few steps toward her, his body mere inches away. "Lovers," he said, his breath tickling her ear.

Splaying her palm against the tree, she closed her eyes and inhaled the strong scent of pine. Lovers. Carving their initials into a tree to proclaim their love. Would she ever feel that way about a man?

An image popped into her head: the smell of wet earth, the feel of hard muscle pressed against her. Soft kisses and long strokes of her hair. She took a deep breath and let the memory penetrate her thoughts. Flesh pressing against flesh, molding, joining. She had loved once. Loved with her body.

"Annie?"

She turned and leaned back against the tree for support, her legs weak, her pulse racing.

"It was you, wasn't it? Here in the forest?" She searched his green eyes.

Hands on his hips, he glanced down at his boots.

"You made love to me," she said.

He didn't answer.

She reached out with her forefinger, and guided his gaze to meet hers. The defiance in his eyes didn't stop her.

"You loved me," she said.

"I'm not capable of love."

"That's not how I remember it."

"Come on. Let's walk around. Maybe you'll remember something else."

He took her wrist and gently tugged. She followed, still dazed by the intensity of the memory. Such beauty, such wonder. And she'd experienced it with Sean.

"How about your guardian? Do you remember him?" he asked.

"An older man? Gray hair?"

"Yep."

"I can see his face, pale blue eyes and a long nose. He wears reading glasses sometimes, I think."

They walked deeper into the woods, twigs snapping beneath their feet. Other images floated to the surface: visiting Raymond's mansion for the first time and feeling like she'd entered a palace. Raymond made her feel treasured for her brains, not ridiculed. He made her feel like a princess.

Darkness fell as Sean headed for a fallen tree. He used it as a bench and sat down. She sat a safe distance away, the damp bark chilling her behind. She shivered.

"Cold?" he asked.

"A little."

"Maybe I've got something in the car." He stood up.

She grabbed his hand. "No. Stay."

Being left in the middle of a dark forest wasn't her idea of fun.

He sat down and placed his arm around her shoulder, pulling her close.

"I shouldn't be doing this," he said.

"Why not?"

"I don't want us to get confused this time."

"Was I confused last time?"

"Kind of."

"Which part do you think I was confused about?"

"Any part that involved me loving you."

"I'm that hard to love?"

"It's not—"

"Don't, I'm starting to get it now. Who would want a freak?" she studied the leaves at her feet.

"You're not a freak."

"Yeah, then why isn't there one person in my life who loves me?"

"That's not true. You've got your mom."

"She has to love me. It comes with the mom contract. And I sense that love wasn't one of my dad's personal strengths. Then there's you…"

She studied the hard lines of his face, the twitch

in his square jaw, as he tipped his head back and blinked at the stars.

"But then you were never real." She sighed. "Maybe losing my memory was the best thing that happened to me."

"Don't say that." He squeezed her shoulder. "You've got a talent for figuring things out that no one else can. It's a gift. Don't turn your back on it."

"And what's your gift, Agent MacNeil?"

"Catching bad guys."

"Come on, I'm serious."

"I don't have any gifts. I'm an average guy."

"I doubt that. There's got to be something that makes you different than all the other FBI agents."

"Not really."

"Hey, if I share, you share. What's your great talent in this world?"

He hesitated. "I guess that would have to be my gut instinct."

She must have looked at him as if he'd grown three heads.

"You know," he paused, "that feeling that something's not right, or something's about to happen."

"I'm not sure I understand."

"When I was a kid and Dad came home drunk, the hair bristled on the back of my neck, warning me. I hid in the attic above my closet. I didn't care about spiders or nails or anything like that. I wasn't going to get a whipping because he'd spent too much of our grocery money on cheap whiskey at McGreevey's."

She didn't know what to say. She wanted to hug him, but knew he'd reject the gesture.

"The old man was good at a lot of things. Gambling his money away, beating his kids, reminding me over and over again how stupid I was."

"I'm sorry," she whispered.

He glanced at her, as if forgetting he told the story out loud.

"Don't be. My instinct saved my ass a lot of times."

He got up and started walking. "Let's go. I think we've both had enough."

She sensed his shame. But why? He hadn't done anything wrong.

Watching him amble up the path, she wondered how anyone could survive that kind of childhood. If there was one thing she knew in her heart, it was that her mom and sisters loved her. Sean didn't think anyone loved him.

"Hey, wait," she said, catching up to him. "What about your mom?"

"What about her?"

"Didn't she do anything? Call police?"

"Forget it. I shouldn't have told you. It serves no purpose."

"But—"

"Please drop it."

He walked her to the passenger side of the car and reached for the door. She blocked him.

"Stop," she said, gripping his arm. What was the matter with her? This wasn't the time to be compassionate about this man's emotional scars. She had her own problems to think about.

"Didn't your mother protect you?" she said.

"She didn't care."

"I don't believe that."

He turned away as if her words physically pained him.

"Sean, talk to me." She touched his cheek.

Recoiling, he grabbed her wrist to break the contact. "It doesn't matter. Dad killed her."

Chapter Nine

Sean hadn't spoken those words since his mom had died seven years ago.

Annie's expression lanced his heart. There could never be anything between them now that she knew what he would become.

"He killed her?" she said.

"He claimed she fell down the basement stairs and broke her neck."

"Maybe she did."

"No. I know the truth. Here." He placed a closed fist to his chest. "Now you know what I really am."

He reached around her and pulled open the door.

"What does your father's behavior have to do with you?" She searched his eyes. He focused on the car seat behind her.

"Please." He motioned toward the car. He couldn't talk about it anymore, couldn't think about it without his insides getting tied in knots.

She got into the car and he shut the door, thanking

God for the steel and glass that separated them, if only for a minute.

He wanted this whole thing over. Wanted Annie safe and Raymond behind bars. He wanted his isolated and routine life back. Only in the future, he'd request assignments that didn't involve getting close to anyone.

"Yeah, right," he muttered, walking around the car. Who was he kidding? The Bureau didn't order him to make Annie fall in love with him. He'd made that decision all by himself.

He slid behind the wheel and pulled away from the shoulder of the road, unable to look at her, afraid of what he'd see in her eyes. Fear? Disgust?

Heading toward the rented cabin, he wondered how on earth she'd gotten that bit of information out of him. He hadn't meant to tell her. No one knew his secret.

Neither of them spoke for twenty minutes. What was she thinking? Did she remember things, but now was afraid to tell him?

"I'd like you to take me in to your superiors." The chill of her voice iced his heart.

"Are you afraid of me?" He had to ask, even if he knew the answer would rip him apart.

"No, not afraid, exactly."

He kept his eyes trained on the road, but felt the heat of her gaze burn his cheek.

"I think it would be best for both of us," she said.

Of course it was. She'd be free of the cold-hearted agent who manipulated her feelings one way, then another.

"If you take me in, maybe they'll help me remember quicker. That's the only way to end this."

He swallowed down a ball of pain rising in his chest. She wanted to end it. To cut him from her life.

Of course she did. He was a monster.

For years, he'd tried to deny the fact that he was a chip off the old block. But it all came crashing down in Chicago when, as a beat cop, he found himself on top of a gangbanger, smashing his face over and over again. The punk had threatened a little kid with a six-inch switchblade. Something snapped. It had taken three cops to pull him off the punk, and a good ten minutes before his heart had stopped racing and his vision had cleared.

That's when he knew he'd become like the old man. That's when he vowed never to let anyone close enough to be burned by the evil pumping through his veins.

A flash caught his eye in the rearview mirror. Blue and white lights.

"Now what?" he muttered.

She looked through the back window, placing her hand between them. So small, so fragile. He struggled not to reach out and touch it, absorb some of its goodness.

"You weren't speeding," she said.

He pulled over and waited, glancing in the rearview mirror. A light went on in the squad car.

"What's he doing?" she asked.

"Checking the plate number."

A few minutes later, the cop approached Sean's side of the car. He rolled down the window.

"License and registration, please." The cop looked barely twenty, with fair skin and light blue eyes. Just his luck to get pulled over by a rookie.

He grabbed the registration from the glove box. "My license was stolen yesterday," he said, not wanting to reveal his identity. "I'm trying to get back home with my wife, and I'll get a new one."

"Did you report it?" The kid scrutinized the registration.

"No, sir, I didn't have time."

The cop nodded and walked back to his car. Sean watched him call dispatch. The light in the patrol car went off. The hair bristled on the back of Sean's neck.

"Something's wrong," he said.

Annie's blue eyes widened. "Why do you say that?"

"I know, that's all." He pulled a wad of fifties from the glove box, scribbled a name and number on the corner of one of the bills, and handed it to her. "It's my buddy's number at the Bureau."

"What are you going to do?"

"I'm not sure yet. It's up to him." He glanced into

the rearview mirror. "Here he comes. If I step out of the car, you get behind the wheel and take off."

"Sean, I—"

"Don't argue about this. You have to believe I know what I'm doing. Okay?" He stared hard into her eyes, wanting to take her in his arms and hold her against him. It was too late for that now.

"What do I tell—"

The cop tapped on her window and she jumped.

"Go ahead, roll it down," Sean said.

She pressed the button and the glass squeaked against the rubber as it slid down. The cop shined a high-powered flashlight in her face.

"Is there a problem, officer?" Sean leaned across her, shielding her body with his own.

"Ma'am, I'm going to have to ask you to get out of the car," the cop said.

"Why?" Sean felt her tremble.

"Sir, I need to talk to the lady." The cop placed his hand to the club at his waist. "Please don't make this difficult."

There was no way in hell Sean was going to let Annie get out of the car alone.

The cop opened her door. Sean pulled her toward him and opened his own door. "Come on, sweetheart."

The endearment, meant to convince the cop of a close relationship with his "wife," rolled off Sean's tongue too easily.

He pulled Annie out of the car to stand beside him. The cop paused in front of her. He was about Sean's height but didn't have a lot of meat on him.

"Are you all right, ma'am?" the cop said. "You look nervous."

She hesitated and Sean held his breath. If she wanted away from him, this was her chance.

"I'm fine." She ran her delicate fingers through her auburn hair. "I was asleep when you pulled us over. I'm kind of out of it."

"I understand. How long have you been married?"

"Five years," she answered without skipping a beat.

"And you live where?"

"Exeter, New Hampshire."

Sean gritted his teeth. She remembered where Raymond kept her locked up as his pet genius. God, it was coming back.

"And what are you folks doing here?" the rookie asked.

"Actually, we were checking out spots for our second honeymoon and we got lost." She cleared her throat. "Sorry, honey. I forgot. You never get lost."

She leaned into Sean's chest and his body tensed.

"These winding roads are hard to navigate," the cop said.

She smiled at him and Sean fisted his hand. In the last forty-eight hours, she hadn't come close to smiling like that at Sean.

"Just the same, you shouldn't be driving without

a license," the cop said. "I'm going to have to ask you to come to the station and fill out a report."

Something flashed in the kid's eyes. There was a lot more happening than a rookie trying to help out tourists.

"I'm tired. Can't we just go home?" she said, taking Sean's arm and yawning.

"It won't take long, ma'am," the cop said. "Why don't you come in the squad car? I wouldn't want you to get lost again."

The kid was cool for a rookie. He obviously needed to bring them in, but wanted to do it with the least amount of resistance. The helpful cop act wasn't a bad approach. It had worked on more than one occasion for Sean.

He led them to the patrol car and opened the back door. She glanced at Sean and slid into the backseat. This was it. Sean coughed, then fell to his knees.

"Sir?" The rookie leaned over to check on him.

He elbowed the kid in the ribs and took him down with a choke hold.

"I don't want to hurt you, kid, so just tell me what this is really about."

"Let go!" the rookie gasped, clawing at Sean's forearm. "I'm a cop!"

"And a pretty good one. But I've been one longer. So let's have it."

The kid bucked and thrashed, but wouldn't give up. Sean applied a little more pressure and the kid passed out.

"Annie, get out of there."

She slid out. "What do we do now?"

Sean cuffed the rookie and dumped him in the backseat.

"We figure out why he really pulled us over." He fingered the paperwork sitting on the front seat and froze.

"Hell."

"What?" She came up behind him. "That's me. Why do they have my picture?"

He scanned the highlights of the bulletin. Zinkerman had been murdered. Suspect: Mary MacNeil, age 27, dark hair, blue eyes, former patient at Appleton. That explained why Zinkerman hadn't shown up at Appleton earlier.

Annie's cheeks paled. With an arm around her shoulder, he led her back to the car.

"They think I killed him?" she squeaked.

"Hatch must have set this up." He eased her into the front seat.

"I'm getting sick of all this." She balled her hands into fists in her lap.

"I know, honey." He clicked her seat belt into place and slid a flyaway strand of hair behind her ear. Damn, he wanted to take her in his arms, hold her, warm her until the emptiness in her eyes was replaced by joy.

Right, and who was he kidding?

Marching to his side of the car, he wondered who

had really killed Zinkerman. He had to admit it was a clever plan, a way to make it nearly impossible for Annie and Sean to escape.

He slid behind the wheel and tore off in anger. Not smart. He didn't want to draw attention to himself.

He glanced at Annie. She stared out the window as if she didn't know where she was.

"Annie, you okay?"

"Peachy." She shot him a fake smile.

His chest ached at the defeat coloring her pale blue eyes.

"We've gotta ditch the car. They've got a description of it in the fax. They've also described me as your companion. We may have to split up."

"No."

She didn't sound happy about it. He couldn't blame her.

"You're going to have to change your appearance," he said.

"Great, I always wanted to be a blonde."

Annie stared out the window, more frustrated than ever. She was wanted for murder? And why should they believe anything she said? She hadn't even been able to remember her own name until Sean had called it out to her.

If she could remember, she could make sense of it all and get some power back. Then, maybe, she would finally be free. That is, if they didn't lock her up for Zinkerman's murder.

"Who do you think killed him?" she said.

"Not sure. The same person who set him up at Appleton? Zinkerman failed to keep you under his control. That was his job."

"He's dead because of me," she said.

"Not because of you. He chose his job, Annie. It's a dangerous business."

"I want no part of it! Cripes, it's bad enough that I awakened from a coma with no memory, that I had to learn to talk and write and eat all over again, but now they think I killed someone. I'm being chased by cops and killers and I can't trust anybody, even you, because you don't really care about me and yet I think I care about you, but I shouldn't care about you because you used me and...argh!" She crossed her arms over her chest. "I want pizza or nachos or cookies."

"O-kay," he said with a smile.

"I sound like an idiot." She closed her eyes and tipped her head back against the seat.

"You sound scared." He paused. "And hungry."

She turned and opened her eyes. "You almost made me smile."

"Almost? I was hoping for a full-blown, round-cheeked smile, like the one you gave that cop back there."

"That was my one smile for the day."

"Too bad."

"Don't you feel daunted by all this?" she said.

"Nope. They're smart but we're smarter. I've got a bona fide genius in my car."

"I don't feel very smart," she said. "I'm terrified."

He placed his hand on her shoulder and squeezed. Heat raced down her arm and danced in her belly. She couldn't even take innocent comfort from this man without her body lighting on fire.

But it wasn't just physical. She wished for her memory back, so she could make sense of her connection to Sean. Maybe she could help him heal from his abused childhood and accept that he was capable of loving.

Loving her.

What on earth was she thinking about now? He wasn't a part of her life and never would be. He'd made it clear he didn't need anyone, that he was destined to be alone.

But Annie sensed those words were spoken by a hurt child who lived inside a damaged man. All he needed was someone to reach out to him, to help him realize it wasn't his fault.

She truly was losing her mind. Five hours ago, she wanted to skip out on the guy. But after the conversation in the forest, she realized Sean was driven by a painful childhood. To think that his own mother didn't protect her son. That she let everything happen around her.

Kind of like me, Annie thought, a feeling of helplessness drifting over her. She remembered going through the motions before, but never really feeling anything. She lived a placid existence, standing outside the bubble of happiness, looking in, but not really feeling.

"Are you remembering something?" he asked.

She glanced at him.

"You got this look on your face," he said. "You used to get that same look when a research project was frustrating the hell out of you."

"Did I like my research?"

"It was your life."

"Didn't that seem odd to you? That a woman of my age would only be interested in lab experiments?"

"I figured it was what you wanted. If you weren't happy, you could have done something about it. Everyone has the power to make choices."

"Not necessarily."

"What do you mean?"

"I'm not sure."

She fidgeted under his scrutiny. She crossed her arms over her chest wondering when they'd both give in and consummate their desire. It was only a matter of time.

They drove a few hours in silence through land rich with pine trees and rolling hills. She struggled against hopelessness that wormed its way into her brain. Her damn brain had started all this. If only she'd been like the other girls, if only she hadn't been smart.

You've got a talent for figuring things out that no one else can. It's a gift. Don't turn your back on it.

Sean's words. Such wisdom and strength from a man who considered himself one step away from being a monster, but she knew differently. Beneath that tortured soul was a kind man.

"There." He pointed to a lake ahead.

"Are we going swimming?"

"No, but the car is."

"I guess this means we're walking."

"To a campground on the other side of the lake. That's where the cabin is. Think you can make it?"

"I guess." Her hip ached in anticipation.

"It's not far. I'd rented a cabin for a week, just in case."

"Just in case?"

"Always have a plan B. I've also got an old truck waiting for us." He parked the car between a thick mass of trees. "I got everything we need in the cabin."

"Food?"

"Yep."

"Cookies? I'd walk a mile for a cookie."

A smile curled the corner of his lips. It fascinated her.

"Come on." He got out of the car and stuffed his pack with supplies from the trunk.

He shifted the car into neutral, and they rolled it into the lake. The car sank into the black mass. Just like that. Erased. As if it had never existed. Kind of like her mind.

"Let's go." He took her hand.

She followed, glancing at their intertwined fingers. If she concentrated on the warmth of his skin, she could block out the fear stalking the recesses of her mind. His hand was firm and solid, and she drew strength from it. Strength she needed to get her to the next step of this nightmare, closer to Mom.

But it wasn't that simple anymore. Now she had to clear her name before she could contact her mother.

They walked. And walked some more. It felt like forever as he shifted his arm around her waist to steady her. They finally approached the perimeter of a campground and he hesitated, taking her hands in his.

"Wait here. I'm going to check out the cabin to make sure it's safe." He handed her his cell phone. "Just in case. I should be back in twenty."

"You said that this morning, and I ended up having to come get you."

"Do not, I repeat, do not come to my rescue this time. Got it?" His eyes flared.

"Hey, you're welcome for saving your butt."

"We were lucky. Promise me if I don't come back, you'll get the hell out of here."

"And abandon my husband?"

"Look, Annie," he started to argue. "Never mind." He started for the cabin. Panic coiled in her tummy.

"Sean?" she whispered after him.

"Yeah?"

She wanted to call out "be careful" or "don't take any chances" or "I love you."

She was completely losing it.

"If you happen to snare a hot dog on your way back, I'd be eternally grateful."

He nodded and disappeared down the trail.

Slumping to a cross-legged position on the ground, she fingered a pinecone. She couldn't love Sean. Not really. She just depended on him for her life. There was a clinical term for that.

"Oh, stop thinking like a scientist," she muttered.

There was something real between them. There had to be. After all, he'd saved her from the assassin, broken into Appleton to get her meds and gone against orders to bring her in, all because he wanted to keep her safe.

Then again, that was his job. Drat.

Staring into the distance, she willed her memory to return.

Images, tastes, smells flared. Sean.

I never thought I could feel this way. Sean's deep, gentle voice.

I love you, Sean.

Just hold me. Make me know it's real.

I'm real. I love you.

The bittersweet taste of merlot on his lips. The scent of his maleness. The feel of his arousal pressing against the bare flesh of her thigh.

"Hey!"

She jumped at the sound of his voice.

"You scared me!" She sprung to her feet.

He put his hand to her shoulder. "You okay? Your cheeks are flushed."

She wanted him to move his hand down, below her jawline, her neck. Beneath her shirt.

"Annie? What is it?"

Her legs felt like oatmeal. "I was just remembering." *And lusting*.

"What?"

"Nothing important."

"Let's get to the cabin," he said. "It's on a back lot, secluded." He took her hand and led her through the darkness along the lake.

"Cabins don't have indoor plumbing, but they've got showers by the ranger station," he said. "I could use one of those."

Sean. Naked. Lathering his lightly haired chest with soap. Running his hands across his stomach and down, washing himself, touching himself.

She stumbled.

"Hey, careful." He steadied her with a hand to her elbow. "The cabin's beyond that clearing."

He kept walking and she was glad he couldn't see her eyes in the darkness. But she wished she could figure out if his words were real or scripted to get close to her and get answers about a mysterious formula.

They approached the cabin, and he shoved a key

into the lock. The door opened with a creak and he flicked the light switch.

"There's canned food in the cabinet over there, maybe even cookies."

She just looked at him.

"I thought you were hungry," he said.

"I am, I was, I…"

He went to her and cupped her shoulders. "What is it?"

"You're going to hurt me again, aren't you?"

Chapter Ten

His chest ached as he let his hands slip from her shoulders. She'd figured it out. Would she run again? He went back to unloading his backpack. He should be relieved that she was wise to him. Instead, he couldn't bear to look at her.

"Sean?"

"Let's get unpacked."

"But—"

He closed the distance between them, but didn't touch her. He couldn't touch her again. "Look, we've got cops and killers on our tails. You should be focusing on changing your appearance and saving your skin, not remembering us, me, whatever."

"You care about me."

"I can't afford to care, not like that. If I do, I'll lose my focus and won't be able to protect you."

"That's what happened before, isn't it?" she said. "I cared too much and you...couldn't allow yourself to care?"

"Please, Annie, we're hungry and tired, and I just can't do this right now."

He turned and she touched his arm. He thought he'd go mad.

"Promise that you won't hurt me again?" she said.

He sighed. "I promise."

What else could he say? If he had to lie to keep her safe, so be it.

"Let's get started on your hair." He pulled supplies from the wooden bureau next to the bed. Scissors, hair color, a comb. He'd stocked the cabin with essentials in case they had to come here.

They should have been sailing away on the *Minerva* by now. But he couldn't risk it. The FBI mole had most likely leaked the location of the boat to Hatch, who would have men waiting for them. Sean hadn't told anyone about the rental cabin back-up plan. He and Annie would be safe, for the time being.

Grabbing the scissors and a towel, he led her to the porch. He fingered her hair, silky soft, brown with hint of copper.

"Lean against the railing." He draped her shoulders with the grayed towel and secured it in front with a tight fold. "Ready?"

He snapped the scissors three times as a warm-up.

"You sure you know what you're doing?"

"Piece of cake. I moonlight as a hairstylist."

She smirked. Well, at last it wasn't a glare of hatred.

He started on the right, pulling her hair straight

down and snipping away with the sharp scissors. Truth was, he'd done this before for his baby sister and had gotten pretty good at it. Four inches of brown hair fell to the wooden porch. She squeaked and shifted to her other foot.

"Stop fidgeting," he said.

"Couldn't I just put it up?"

"Too late. I've cut one side. Can't have you going around lopsided. That would definitely attract attention."

Another squeak escaped her lips.

He cut straight across the back and around to the left side.

"Almost done." His fingers brushed against her neck. Her skin felt so warm against his knuckles.

He finished the blunt cut just above her shoulders and stepped around to face her. "How about bangs?"

"Do I have a choice?"

"Would be a completely different look for you."

"Yeah, I'll look like I'm twelve."

"Not with a little eye makeup. I've got some of that, too."

"I'll look like a twelve-year-old delinquent."

"Have a little faith."

He combed her bangs down over her forehead.

"What was Raymond like?" she asked.

It was a good thing she couldn't see his eyes. "He's rich and powerful." He sandwiched a section of hair between two fingers.

"You don't like him?" she said.

He snipped at her bangs, making a straight line across her forehead.

"Not especially."

"Why?"

"I don't trust him."

"I don't trust you," she shot back.

"Yet you're letting me cut your hair," he joked.

She actually smiled. A minute passed and he ran the comb through her hair. She closed her eyes.

"Do you think we stand a chance against the bad guys?" she said.

"We stand a very good chance. Okay, open your eyes."

She did, and the clearest shade of blue stared back at him. Blue eyes filled with hope, peppered with fear.

"You'll be okay, Annie," he said, brushing his thumb against her cheek.

They stood there, rooted in place for a good minute. He couldn't move, mesmerized by the desperate look in her eyes.

"You wouldn't lie to me, would you?" she said.

"No." His heart shattered. Maybe he should spill the whole truth, including how he had fallen for her before—had fallen fast and hard—and how he'd promised himself not to let it happen again.

Who was he kidding?

She ran her fingers through her hair. "Well? How do I look?"

"What?" He didn't understand the question.

"My hair? How do I look?"

Good enough to kiss.

"Good. Now for the color."

He brushed past her and went inside, wanting to get away from the temptation of her lips. He couldn't stand much more of this. No matter how she looked, or how he'd butchered her hair, her eyes drew him in.

Grabbing the box of hair dye, he sat at the kitchen table and mixed the color.

"So, tell me the truth, am I going to end up with green hair?" she said from the doorway.

"Let's hope not. That would really draw attention to you." He motioned to the chair on the other side of the table. She crossed her arms over her chest and stared him down. His body lit with need.

"I'm not sure about this." She ambled to the table and flopped down in the chair. She crossed one leg over the other, both hands gripping the armrests.

He put on the latex groves and got started.

"I suppose next you're going to have me pierce my nose," she said.

"Actually, that's not a bad idea."

She glared. "You wouldn't."

"It would completely change your look."

"And what about your look? Are you dying your hair purple?"

"Nah." He massaged the dye into her scalp. "I've

got a fake mustache and glasses. Even have a wig, if I need it."

Finishing the last few strands of hair, he blocked out her squeaks of pleasure as he massaged her scalp. He took a step back and ripped the gloves from his hands, tossing them into the trash.

"Now we wait," he said. "Twenty minutes, maybe twenty-five."

Kneeling, he placed a few logs in the fireplace and balled up old editions of the *Moosehead Messenger* newspaper for kindling. He stuffed them between the logs.

Annie's chair legs scratched against the wood floor. She was closing in on him. He could feel it.

"So." She placed a hand to his shoulder. "FBI by day, hairdresser by night. Amazing."

"That's not the half of it," he joked.

"Tell me," she said.

He glanced over his shoulder, but couldn't speak. Enough. He could not reveal any more of himself to her. It had to stop here.

"We need more wood." He got up and went to the door. "Lock it behind me. I've got the key."

"But you said we're safe out here." She hugged her midsection.

"Relatively safe. We've always got to be on guard."

He closed the door, waiting until he heard the click of the lock. Stepping off the porch, he paced into the darkness, but not too far. He'd never be far away from her again. But right now he needed some space, breathing room to get his perspective back.

Her vulnerability, her trust and her fear, all made him want to take her in his arms. They couldn't get mixed up this time. They had to keep it strictly professional.

Not wanting to be caught in a lie, he went around to the back of the cabin and pulled a few logs from a pile he'd stocked. He was glad he'd rented this place as a backup. It was turning out to be an excellent safe house.

A shriek echoed from the cabin and he tossed the logs aside. Racing up the porch steps, he realized he'd left his weapon in the cabin. Once again, his emotions had put her life in danger.

He took a deep breath, unlocked the door and went inside. The cabin was empty.

His blood ran cold. Grabbing his firearm, he scanned the room. No sign of a struggle.

Panic drummed a frantic beat in his head. Annie...gone. He wouldn't lose her like this. Sweat beaded in his palms.

A car door slammed. He raced outside and collided with her in the darkness.

"I look like a freak!" She cried, her voice echoing through the pine trees.

"Shhh, calm down."

"Look at my hair."

He could barely see the color in the dark. "Let's go inside."

"I want this off my hair, now!"

"The water pump's over there. I'll get some shampoo."

He went into the cabin and got supplies. She was okay, everything would be okay.

"Are you coming?" she cried.

He brought her the shampoo and stood by as she yanked the water pump.

"It doesn't work. I can't get any water," she said.

Still coming off an adrenaline rush, he wasn't sure if he should hold her or lecture her for scaring the hell out of him.

He decided to pump water. She rinsed her hair and then lathered up, mumbling under her breath.

"You scared the hell out of me," he said.

She snapped her head up. "I can see why. This," she motioned to her hair, "would scare the hell out of anybody."

She snatched the conditioner and squeezed it into her hair. He pumped and she rinsed.

"I hate this," she said. "I don't want to look like someone else." She straightened and grabbed the towel off his shoulder. "I want to be me. Just Annie. Not a scientist, not a key to some federal investigation. Just Annie."

She headed for the cabin and he followed. She'd always been so quiet and mild-mannered before, so accepting and polite.

Then again, her life was being torn apart.

She turned on him. "Just Annie. Who is that, anyway? Does anybody know?"

He did. Annie was a compassionate, clever girl who'd discovered a vaccine for a rare virus created by another scientist on Raymond's payroll. Raymond hoped Annie's vaccine would start a bidding war between pharmaceutical companies. Everything was about money and power to that bastard. The FBI had to nail him before he unleashed the virus in his strategy to pressure the drug companies.

"You going to shoot someone?" she said, glancing at the gun he'd shoved into his waistband.

"Wasn't sure," he said. "I heard you scream. The cabin was empty. Didn't know what happened."

"I'm having an attack." She marched toward the porch.

"Annie?"

She turned and stared him down. "What?"

"What prompted all this?"

"What difference does it make? It won't help to talk about it."

"You remembered something, didn't you?"

She stared at the ground, her hands planted firmly on her hips.

"Talk to me," he said.

She glanced up, her eyes pleading with his soul. If only he could heal what he saw there. If only—

"I hate this." She raced into the cabin.

He stared after her, realizing his heart hadn't recovered its normal beat. She was okay. Everything was going to be okay.

He went inside and found her pacing from the window to the bed and back again.

"I've always done the right thing," she said. "I was a good girl. I remember that. Well, maybe I don't want to be good anymore. Maybe I just want to be honest."

"Meaning what?"

"I hate my father."

The honesty of her confession felt like a sucker punch to his gut. Shame. He'd felt it himself.

"I feel like a jerk for saying it, but I truly hate him. I remember the day he left. He drove off in his beat-up Chevy. Then, years later, he came looking for money. Thank God Raymond's driver was with me that day."

He glanced at the floor, hating the sound of gratitude in her voice when she spoke of Raymond.

"Dad tried to talk me into leaving Raymond." She paced to the window and back. "I thought he came back because he missed me and wanted us to be a family. I remember standing outside of school and rambling about how happy Mom would be when we were together again. What a fool."

She paced to the window and stared outside. The best thing for her was to let go of the memories and the pain so she could finally be free, he thought. He should take his own advice.

"My father saw an opportunity to make money off his little girl by using my intelligence to help him win at the track. My own father…"

"Just because they're our parents doesn't mean they love us." The words slipped from his lips.

"I guess I was lucky to have Raymond," she whispered. "Someone who cared."

He fisted his hand in his pocket. She was remembering, all right. Bits and pieces. The long-ago past before the most recent past. But she didn't remember it all. She didn't realize how deep the betrayal went in her life.

"But Dad wasn't the only one. Other people let me down. But I can't seem to access it all." She pounded a closed fist against the wooden table. "Why can't I remember?"

"What's your instinct telling you?"

"I don't have instinct or I wouldn't have been fooled so many times by people I thought loved me."

His gut clenched. Sean was tops on that list.

"You've got instincts, Annie," he said, taking a step toward her, then another. "You have to learn how to tap into them."

"I don't believe in instinct. I believe in concretes, methodology and equations. Things I can touch and feel." She paced to the window and back to the fireplace. "If I could get my hands on my lab equipment, I know I could stimulate my memory."

"Even I'm not that good."

"What?" She turned to him.

"To break into your lab."

"But you agree it could work?"

"Probably. That's why I took you to the forest."

"And I remembered things, flashes of the past. We need to…" She hesitated and her eyes widened. "We need to make love."

"What?"

"We did that before, right? A few times?"

"Yeah, but, I don't know, Annie." He sat on the wooden bench, his legs suddenly weak. He didn't know if he could do it, didn't know if he could make love to her without losing his last shred of integrity.

"You took me back to the forest to help me remember. I think if we re-create an intense scene, it might all come back."

Re-creating a scene. That's all it was. It wasn't as if she wanted to make love to him because she loved him. She was a scientist who'd figured out a way to reach her goal: remembering so she could get away from him.

"Are you sure?" he said.

"I know the thought probably isn't all that appealing. I mean, I'm not the most beautiful-looking woman on the face of the earth right now."

"No, that's not it." He went to her and took her chin between his forefinger and thumb, guiding her gaze to meet his. He couldn't stop himself from wanting to drive the pain from her eyes. The pain of not knowing herself.

Slipping one hand into her hair, he brought his mouth down to hers. Her lips trembled and he wondered if she really wanted to do this, or if she was sacrificing herself for her memory's sake.

No, he wouldn't have her that way. He broke the kiss.

"Annie," he hushed, his breath heavy against the softness of her cheek. "I don't want to hurt you."

"Then help me," she said, out of breath.

She reached for him then, pulling gently on the back of his neck. The kiss was desperate and hot, her lips claiming him, heart and soul.

They stumbled a few steps and fell onto the wool-blanketed double bed. Sprawled across him, her fingers threaded through his hair. Damn, that felt good. Then her tongue flitted across his lips, soft as a feather, coaxing his response. He resisted at first, not knowing why. But he couldn't deny her anything, even a part of his soul.

Somewhere in the recesses of his mind, he felt her fingers strip him of his flannel shirt.

She was in charge. As it should be. He wouldn't take advantage of her. This time, she would be the one to decide how she wanted it and for how long. Hell, if she changed her mind at the last minute, he would accept it, although every nerve ending in his body would ache with wanting.

He felt his undershirt pulled free from the waist-band of his jeans. She wasn't going to stop; she was determined to recreate their lovemaking right here, right now.

She placed his hands above him on the pillow, and he kept them there, humbling himself before her.

The way her hands slipped beneath his shirt and crawled up his stomach to his chest, it was obvious this woman knew exactly what she wanted. He couldn't believe she wanted it from him.

She broke the kiss, and he searched her eyes. What did she want him to do?

"Your shirt." She breathed heavy as she spoke. "It's in the way."

She slipped the shirt over his head and straddled him. She shucked her sweater and peeled the knit blouse over her head to reveal bare flesh, perfectly shaped breasts with pebbled nipples. He reached out and cupped them, running his thumb over each hardened peak. She moaned and arched against him, her eyes fluttering closed.

"God, Annie." He couldn't believe how her body responded to his touch. Her hips rocked forward and his hand slipped beneath her panties until his fingers found the right spot.

"Sean, do something," she begged.

"Lean against me."

She pressed her warm breasts against his chest, sending a wave of need coursing through his body.

He slipped her pants from her hips and down. Laying featherlight kisses against his neck, Annie shimmied and kicked until she was naked.

She unsnapped his jeans and his body lit on fire from her anxious touch. He automatically lifted his hips, and she stripped him of everything from the waist down, revealing the intensity of his desire.

He wanted her more than he'd wanted anything. But did he deserve her?

Rubbing against him, his heat brushed her thigh and she cried out in agony, or nirvana, he wasn't sure which. All he knew was that the friction of skin against skin, the soft touch of her tongue against his neck, was driving him insane.

"Annie." Her name escaped his lips, but was silenced by her lips pressing against his, softly, gently.

Whatever she wanted, whatever she'd do to him, Sean wouldn't resist.

"Make love to me," she said against his lips. "Love me like this is the only day."

He couldn't wait. Gripping her backside, he pulled her against him. She let out a squeak and Sean searched her eyes, but they were closed with passion. She bit her lower lip as her hips moved forward, then back.

With open palms she pressed against his chest and sat up, tipping her head back, arching her back. Her hips moved slowly, driving Sean out of his mind. How long could he stay just outside the gates of ecstasy?

Then she thrust forward, taking him in, absorbing him completely.

Annie wanted him. Like before, only different. She wasn't being tricked or manipulated into making love to him this time.

"Sean, please," she begged.

Her fingers pinched his skin with such desperation, such need. With a moan from deep in his chest, he thrust one last time and the world exploded.

She collapsed against him, their bodies still joined. Never in his life had he felt such trust with another human being. Never had he needed someone like he needed Annie.

He stroked her back as she lay on top of him. Her skin soft, her breath warm against his shoulder.

Sean needed her.

And she needed to remember.

Yet once she did, she'd realize what he'd done. She'd remember the darkness in his eyes that cold February night. Only an insane woman could love such a man.

Dread swirled in his gut. It was a matter of minutes, maybe seconds, before she put it all together and cut him loose.

The steady beat of her heart drummed against his chest, a connection that pulsed from deep in his soul. Did their lovemaking spark her memory?

She gazed into his eyes. Lingering passion

simmered there. Passion and something else. It couldn't be.

"Well, we do that like expert married folks," she said.

He stilled at the thought of being married, of sharing the rest of his life with her.

"But I've got a confession to make," she said.

"What?"

"It didn't work."

Hell, it had worked just fine for him. "Sorry. You didn't enjoy it?"

"I mean it didn't jog my memory."

"Oh." He glanced away, reality slapping him in the face. She didn't make love to him for physical pleasure or emotional satisfaction. It was a method by which to remember and gain her freedom.

"There's only one thing to do," she said.

"What, take you in?"

"Nope." She straddled him and smiled. "Keep trying."

Chapter Eleven

Annie stretched like a cat waking from a deep sleep. Reaching out, she ached to warm her fingertips against the heat of Sean's skin. Instead, her fingers brushed across starched cotton.

She sat up, holding the sheets to her breasts. She was alone. Sunshine filtered through the sheer window coverings. A chill swept through the cabin. Their temporary sanctuary seemed colder than last night.

Had he left because he was ashamed? Regretted their lovemaking?

She didn't. She could still feel his hands on her body, trailing down her rib cage to her hips, cupping her behind, sending her skyrocketing to the stars. No ordinary man could make her feel this way.

Only the man she loved had that kind of power.

No, it couldn't be.

She opened her eyes and stared at the wood-beamed ceiling. Now what kind of mess had she gotten herself into?

The door burst open, and she pulled the covers to her chest.

"You're awake," he said in a voice softer than his usual tone.

He dumped two large plastic bags on the table and rummaged through them.

"I went outside to make a call. Didn't want to wake you," he said, not making eye contact. He was obviously uncomfortable about last night. "I've got good news." He glanced at her and cleared his throat. "I talked to my boss. He checked with the medical team and they said you could probably up your dose of meds by one a day to help with your memory disorder."

Her heart sank. That's what this was about. Remembering.

"I'll remember everything, then?" she said, wishing she could remember what scared him so much that he kept her at a safe distance.

"You'll remember."

She could have sworn regret colored his voice.

"Here." He offered her a pill and a glass of water. "You'll take the other one at dinner."

"I need to ask you something," she said, then swallowed the pill.

"Yeah?"

"Tell me why you're so scared."

"I tend to get that way when I'm being hunted by hired killers."

He ambled over to the fireplace and knelt down, poking at the logs with a stick.

"Did I do something to you?" she asked.

He glanced over his shoulder. "What do you mean?"

"Did I hurt you or betray you in some way?"

"It was nothing like that." He glanced back at the fire.

"Then, what?"

"You need a shower."

"Oh?"

"I didn't mean it like that. I meant—"

"Forget it. I could use a bathroom." She could tell he wasn't going to spill his guts this morning.

He got up and pulled a sweatshirt and pants from a bag. "Here." He tossed them at her.

The sweatshirt had a pine tree on the front. "Stylish," she joked.

"I'll wait outside."

She hopped from the warm bed and quickly dressed, then looked through the supplies. Toothbrush, floss, mild soap and baby powder. She'd used that before. And Sean remembered.

She opened the door and spied him leaning casually against the cabin.

"Ready?"

"Sure."

They walked side by side to the showers, neither of them speaking. What should she say? "Hey, I love you, you big idiot and I know you love me?"

She had a feeling he wouldn't respond well to the direct approach. She blushed at the memory of the things they'd done to each other last night, naughty and wonderful things. Things she never thought possible.

"Here's the ladies' bathroom." Sean paused in front of a brown metal door. "The campground isn't full, but there are a few folks around. Don't make eye contact with anyone. Blend in, like you're part of the scenery."

She pushed through the squeaky door. No showers were going. Good. Annie relieved herself, then made her way to a shower. She placed her supplies on the wooden bench in the shower stall, hung her towel on the hook, and flipped on the water.

It would feel good to cleanse the past few days off her body, she thought, sticking her hand under the water to test its temperature. Although she was reluctant to cleanse her body of the lingering scent of sex that permeated each and ever pore.

When the temperature was just right, she stripped off the sweatpants and shirt and stepped under the heavy spray. She lathered her body with soap, remembering the tingling sensation coursing through her body when Sean had stroked her skin with his large hands. Would they make love again? Or was the question *when* would they make love again?

She washed her hair, her body weak yet rejuvenated from their lovemaking. She was alive again, completely alive. She hoped she felt this way for a long time.

She wanted to stay beneath the shower's pounding spray for hours. Instead, she rinsed her hair and body as quickly as possible. She turned off the water and froze at the sound of metal scraping against metal.

Someone was outside her changing stall. She wrapped her arms around her midsection, fighting to quell the panic. She felt his presence, felt him leering at her from the other side of the curtain, ready to strike. Goose bumps crawled across her body. She was cold and scared. Naked and vulnerable.

She hated the feeling. Hated the grating fear that rooted her in place. She grabbed her towel and wrapped it around her body.

"Sean?" she said, hoping it was him on the other side of the curtain.

Silence answered her. Fear paralyzed her, then anger took hold. She was done being controlled by fear. If she was going to die right here, then so be it. But it wouldn't be without a fight.

Grabbing a brush in one hand and a small can of deodorant spray in the other, she readied for battle. Maybe a quick whack to the head or squirt in the eyes would stun her assailant long enough for her to get help.

A click reverberated off the walls. She swallowed her fear and forged ahead.

"I'm sick of this!" she cried and swung at the curtain, whipping it aside. The bathroom was empty.

"Annie?" Sean cracked open the bathroom door, then raced in to help her. "My God, Annie? What is it?"

Gripping her shoulders, he searched her eyes. "What happened?"

"Someone was…here." She didn't recognize the sound of her own voice. "Outside the shower."

"You're fine. You're fine." He unwrapped the towel from her body and dried off her shoulders, then her hair. "I was right outside. No one came in here but a mom and her kid. Maybe the kid went wandering around. You're safe."

She pressed her face into his thick sweatshirt and interlaced her hands around his waist. When he said the words, she felt safe in his arms.

"Let's get you dressed."

Shaking from the chill or fear, she clung to him for warmth. "One more minute."

He squeezed her tight and she took a few deep breaths. His scent somehow calmed her.

"Okay," she said, pushing away.

With trembling fingers, she reached for her sweatshirt. He grabbed it and slipped it over her head, then helped her with her sweatpants and socks. Funny. His touch felt different than last night, firm and unshakable, as opposed to tentative and humbled.

She needed unshakable right now. She needed him to be the Rock of Gibraltar instead of the sexiest man of the year. He motioned for her to sit down on the bench. He knelt in front of her and tied her sneakers.

He gathered the supplies. "Let's go."

She clung to him, wrapping her arms around his

waist and hooking her fingers into the belt loops of his jeans. He walked her to the door and peeked out.

"It's clear." He opened the door and guided her to the gravel path that led to their cabin.

"You think I'm crazy, don't you?" she said.

"Nope."

"I heard someone."

"You're okay now."

They approached the cabin and she berated herself for being paranoid. It was her overactive imagination. The last forty-eight hours had been emotionally exhausting. And she was hungry.

Sean unlocked the door and led her inside. He went to the fireplace and started a fire. She ambled to the kitchen table, grabbed a box of mini muffins and sat down.

"Look," she said. "Last night didn't do what I'd hoped it would."

Boy, was that an understatement.

"And I can't stand waiting for morsels of the past to come floating back. You've got to help me."

"You're supposed to remember on your own." He sat across the table from her. "The psychologists said—"

"Forget the psychologists." She touched his hand and thought he'd pull away, but he didn't. "Tell me about us. I can't stand not knowing, waiting for something to jump out the shadows and snatch away the one thing that makes me happy."

His eyes widened. "I…make you happy?"

"What do you think?" She leaned over and kissed him; she couldn't help herself. His lips looked so perfect, soft and full. And she wanted to taste him again. One night of passion was not enough.

He pushed her away and got to his feet. "Don't, Annie. This can't happen again."

"What?"

"Us. Any of this." He wiped the back of his hand across his lips, and her heart cracked.

"Talk to me," she demanded.

He paced to the front door.

"Don't you dare run from me again," she said.

He turned and stared her down. "It's you who should be running. I'm just like the rest. I used you, Annie. Tricked you into falling in love with me because I needed information. It was all about the job, about catching the bastards who were trying to buy and sell your research."

"I don't believe you."

"You always were naive."

"Bastard," she spit out.

"Yeah, that's good. That's what I am and don't you forget it."

"I don't buy it." She stood. "You're terrified, and not of the killers out to get me. It's something else."

"Don't you get it? You were my assignment," he said, staring into her eyes. "Get close to you, find out everything I could about the formula."

No, it couldn't be. "There's more, isn't there?"

Tell me there's more. Tell me you fell in love with me.

"Sure, there's more." He shoved his hands into his pockets. "I caused your accident."

She took a step back. "What?"

"I caused you to freak out and drive off. You don't know how to drive. No wonder you drove over that cliff. I could have stopped you. I didn't. I didn't have the guts to face up to what I was: a bastard who'd chewed you up and spit you out like a piece of tobacco. I didn't care about you. I didn't care that you'd fallen in love with me. You get it now?"

"No." She took another step back, her mind racing, trying to remember. She had to remember.

"Face it. I'm like your dad. I used you like he did when he came back. Hell, last night was a way to get you to remember."

The crackling of the fire grew to a fevered pitch in her ears, drowning out all sound, all words he aimed at her. But they hit hard, like daggers to her chest.

What does your heart tell you? It was her mother's voice.

Her heart? Did she still have one?

"So, don't go thinking you can trust me," he shouted. "Because I'll break your heart—Annie!"

He yanked her away from the fire, snatched a blanket from the bed and swung it at her pants.

"You're on fire. Didn't you feel it?"

Feel it? Hell, she wasn't sure she had any feeling left after his verbal lashing.

Didn't love her, didn't care about her. Used her like everyone else. Only wanted her for her brains.

She vaguely felt him guide her to the bed, her mind a daze of past, present and pain.

"Sit down. I'll get the first aid kit."

He disappeared and she found herself staring into the fire, its flames bright and bold, hypnotizing her.

She wasn't one to feel sorry for herself. She hated the sound of her voice before, condemning her father, condemning the other, faceless people in her life who had used and betrayed her. And now she knew the truth: Sean was one of them.

"Here." He lifted her leg to rest on the bed. She stared into the fire, its heat burning a path all the way to her heart. Anger. Frustration. Pain.

She closed her eyes.

His hands, so gentle, so tender, touched her skin like a father touching a newborn babe. Trailing up one side of her calf, soft and soothing. It didn't make sense. A monster wouldn't touch her like this.

Follow your heart.

Sean had called it instinct. Her mother called it following your heart. And Annie knew there was more to this man than his hurtful words.

"It barely got the skin, but I'll put something on it to be safe," he said, rubbing ointment on her leg.

He grasped her calf between his hands as if he were holding a delicate piece of crystal. He must care. Someone who didn't care wouldn't take such good care of her. It didn't make sense. But then, sometimes relying on the facts didn't always get you where you wanted to go.

Follow your heart.

She studied his face, concern creasing his features as he focused on her leg. He looked pained himself.

"You're a liar," she said.

He glanced up, and her heart caught at the emptiness in his eyes.

"Yeah, and then some," he said. "I'm a violent, controlling man. I've grown up like the old man, only thinking of myself, only caring about myself."

She glanced at her leg, then into his eyes. "Really?"

He propped her leg gingerly to a pillow and walked to the table where he tossed the jar of ointment into his backpack.

Follow your heart.

"I'm not buying it, MacNeil," she said.

"Don't be a fool. I told you how I used you."

"But you didn't tell me all of it, did you?" she pushed.

"I told you all you need to know. Now let me do my job and stay away from me so you won't get hurt again."

"What aren't you telling me?"

"There's nothing more to tell. Go to sleep or something."

"I'd sleep better with you."

"Stop, damn it." He turned and stared her down.

"Why?"

"Because we can never be. Nothing good can come of this."

"I disagree."

"Look at your leg." He marched over and pointed at her calf. "I did this. I came at you until you backed into a fire and didn't even feel the burn. I'm a bastard just like—"

"You're not him."

He took a step back, his eyes radiating horror.

"That's what you're afraid of, isn't it?" she said. "That you'll become your father?"

"I've already become him." He paced the small cabin, running his hand through rich, dark hair. His heavy step caused the hardwood planks to creak.

"You're nothing like him," she said.

"You don't know what you're talking about."

"I'm the one you've been taking care of these past few days, remember?"

"It's my job."

"That's all?"

"That's all."

She hated doing it, but somehow she had to make him see what this was really about. Who he really was.

"Fine, you're right. You're a bastard and I don't need your help." She got to her feet. "Where are the keys?"

"Why?"

"I'm leaving."

"What are you talking about? See you never used to do stuff like this. Never put yourself at risk."

"Hey, according to you, I'm at risk right now. You're a bastard and I should stay away from you." She searched his backpack for keys.

"You're not going anywhere." His deep voice sent shivers across her shoulders.

"If I'm as smart as everybody thinks I am, I can take care of myself."

"That's my responsibility."

She took a fortifying breath. "Well, if I must say so, you've done a pretty mediocre job. Let's see. I've had to save your butt twice in the last three days. Maybe I should be the FBI agent."

His jaw twitched, but she didn't back down. She remembered his incoherent ramblings the other night at the motel.

"But then Eddy always said you were stupid, didn't he? He knew you'd never amount to much."

His eyes widened. She could tell he struggled to maintain his composure.

She took four steps toward him. "But you were smart enough to manipulate my feelings. You had me wrapped around your finger, and yet you never felt anything. Boy, that must have been fun. Was it fun, Sean?" she said, jabbing at his chest with an open palm. He backed up against the wall.

"You don't understand," he said, his voice like ice.

"Was it a thrill breaking a naive young woman's heart? Did you enjoy it?"

She closed in on him, their bodies nearly touching.

His green eyes burned with rage; his lids fell to half-mast as if steeling himself from her assault.

"I'll bet you enjoyed breaking my heart like your old man enjoyed breaking your mother's body, limb by limb." She felt his breath warm her skin. "Like you want to do to me now. You want me out of your face, don't you? Well, I'm not going anywhere. Not unless you move me."

Her heart ached at the pain in his eyes. But she wasn't afraid of his anger. She knew this was the only way.

"Come on, tough guy." She shoved at his chest. Once. Twice. On the third shove, he grabbed her wrists and squeezed tight.

But not too tight. They stared into each other's eyes. Her heart pounded in her ears.

"What are you trying to do?" he rasped.

"Love you."

He released her wrists and dropped his hands to his sides as if in surrender.

"Let it go," she said.

"What?"

"The fear of becoming your father. The self-control that you wear like steel around your heart."

"I can't. It's the only thing that keeps me from being like him. It's my salvation."

"It's your jailer. It keeps you from feeling, from living."

"It keeps me from hurting," he said.

"You're hurting now."

"I've gotta get out of here." He pushed past her and started for the door.

"Coward." She grabbed a ceramic mug and threw it, hitting him squarely in the back.

"What the—" He spun around and she threw a toothbrush, then a box of matches. He blocked them with his hands.

"Run away, coward. Go on." She picked up a log.

"Put it down," he said.

"Or what? You're going to stop me from throwing it?"

She wielded it over her shoulder, ready to let it fly. In three strides, he pinned her to the wall and swiped the log from her hands.

"What do you want from me, Annie?"

"I want you to be honest. I want you to let go."

"Meaning what? You want me to bare my heart and soul to you?" He tossed the log beside the fireplace. "You want me to describe in graphic detail how my father beat us and bought off the local cops whenever they came around?"

He stormed to the table and gripped the edges with shaky fingers. "I had to control myself to keep from giving him the satisfaction. Each time he hit me, belittled me for being stupid, I sucked it in and didn't show an ounce of emotion."

"But you felt it."

"I don't feel anything. Just like him."

"Is that right?" Anger coiled in her gut.

"Face it, you fell in love with a heartless bastard before the accident."

"That's not who I'm in love with now."

He spun around. "Don't say that."

"What? That I love you?"

"Don't. You couldn't possibly love me."

"Why not?"

"Because, all right?"

"Let it go."

"Damn it, stop saying that!" he cried, flipping over the kitchen table. The backpack and bags of supplies crashed to the floor.

It was a good start.

"I hate the bastard!" He kicked at the table, then reached for the chair and tossed it across the room. It crashed against the wall and fell on its side. "I don't want the old man's damn legacy!"

"He's a son of a bitch!" she encouraged, snatching a pillow from the double bed.

"I never wanted to be like him!" He pounded his fists against the wall. She tossed the pillow at him and he swung at it, sending feathers shooting across the room. Some clung to his hair.

"I wanted…" He threw the pillow to the bed and punched it dead center. Again. And again.

"You wanted what?"

"I wanted them—" he continued punching "—to love me."

He pushed away from the bed and slid to the floor, the deflated pillow clutched between his fingers.

She sat cross-legged next to him. Feathers dotted his hair; his cheeks were flushed red, either from anger or embarrassment.

But she was sure of one thing. She'd proven her point: letting go was a completely healthy experience, not a violent one that would hurt someone he loved.

"How do you feel?" she said.

"Confused."

"Why?" She plucked a white feather from his hair.

"Because all I can think about right now is making love to you."

Her breath caught at the need in his eyes.

"Why does that confuse you?"

"Look at what I just did. I lost it, I trashed the place, I—"

"You peeled away some of that crud around your heart. You needed to do that."

He glanced into the burning embers, the flames dancing in the reflection of his eyes. She reached out and touched his cheek with her fingertips. He blinked and looked at her, his green eyes tinged with confusion yet brimming with desire.

"Now there's room in your heart for me." She brushed her lips against his, then guided his cheek to her chest. His arms naturally wrapped around her midsection.

This felt right and safe. And real.

"Thanks," he said.

She stroked his hair. "Sure."

With one last kiss to her cheek, he stood and extended his hand. She took it and he pulled her to her feet, their bodies close, on fire.

"How about some coffee?" he said.

"I'll make it." She broke contact, needing some space to catch her breath.

She loved him. And she was pretty sure he loved her.

"You don't know how to make coffee," he said.

"Wanna bet?"

Digging through the box of supplies, she found a metal tin of instant coffee. She slipped off the top, cool against her fingers.

A flash popped in her brain like a strobe light. The can should be empty. Something inside. Heart racing. Couldn't be caught.

"Oh, my God!"

Chapter Twelve

Sean gripped her shoulders. Damn, was she going to pass out again? Had the medical team given him the wrong advice by having her up her dosage of medication?

"Annie?" he said. "What is it?"

She emptied the contents of the tin onto the table. "It was empty. I put something inside. About an inch long, some kind of mini hard drive, I think."

"Okay, sit down, breathe." He needed her to remember and figure out who Raymond was, who Sean was. His heart skipped with panic. No, it was okay now. She knew it all, yet still loved him. He could feel it.

She pulled out her journal and scribbled notes. This could do it. If she remembered where she had hidden the formula, they could get it to the proper authorities. Once the formula was in the government's hands, she'd be safe.

He paced to the window. But where did that leave

his case? He had nothing on Raymond Phelps unless he could link him to the formula. Somehow that didn't mean as much as keeping Annie safe.

That was a first, he admitted, staring outside at the peaceful trees. Putting away the bad guys had been his driving force for the last ten years. Locking them up, making sure they couldn't hurt anyone.

He'd be damned if he'd let Phelps get within a hundred feet of Annie.

"Damn!" she cried, slamming the pen to the table.

"What's wrong?" He massaged her shoulders.

"It's making sense. I'm remembering what works and what doesn't. But it's like there's this blind spot where something's hidden. And it's the weirdest thing…"

He guided her gaze to meet his. "What's weird, sweetheart?"

"I think Mom's got it."

"What do you mean?"

She clutched the coffee tin. "Why would Mom have the formula? That makes no sense." She shrugged. "Maybe I'm losing my mind," she muttered, placing the tin on the table. "Damn, it's so close."

"Annie?"

"What?"

"We'd better go see your mom."

Her eyes widened. "Are you sure?"

"You need to remember it all. If your mom holds the key, then that's where we'll go."

She nodded and hugged him with such abandon.

He wanted to stay this way forever, wrapped in her warmth.

She pushed away from him. "But it's dangerous."

"Not if we do it right. On our own. If we run into any trouble, I'll handle it."

"I'm going to see Mom. And the farm, I remember the farm. Pigs and horses and cats. We had tons of cats," she said, stuffing clothes into the pack.

"We shouldn't meet her there. We probably shouldn't call her, either."

"We could be waiting for her in one of the vacation homes she cleans. She does Millerstown homes on Tuesdays, I remember that. I used to go with her sometimes. She'd make up these silly songs..." her voice drifted off.

He held her in his arms. "You'll see her soon. We'll end this, nail the bad guys and you can go back home."

He let go and headed for the door. "I'm going to do a once-over on the truck. The farmer who sold it to me said it guzzles oil."

"Sean?"

He glanced at her.

"Thanks," she said.

If she only knew how much he had to thank her for.

He closed the door and Annie stared at the worn oak. They were taking a big chance by going to see Mom.

He'd taken an even bigger one earlier. He'd given in to the pain, trusted her enough to let go and become completely vulnerable. He trusted her, maybe even loved her.

She scooped a pillow from the floor and tossed it to the bed. She couldn't stand the thought of Sean doing this alone and risking his life to protect her. She'd found love, joined with a man who completed her. She wasn't about to lose him. And as a fugitive, Annie was putting Mom in danger, as well.

They needed help, but Sean said he couldn't trust the FBI. There had to be someone who could help, someone powerful and trustworthy.

She spied Sean's cell phone on the kitchen table. "Of course," she whispered.

THE DRIVE TO Millerstown was the longest three hours of her life. They waited in the musty basement of the Pinewood Cabin, the place Mom kept her supplies, and her first stop every Tuesday morning.

Sitting on the cellar steps, she remembered the first time her mother had brought her here when she was seven. Annie was fascinated with the old library hidden in the basement, filled with books about so many interesting things: cell structure, protists, the animal kingdom. Her choice of subject matter was evidence that Annie was different, smarter than the average seven-year-old.

Sean paced the damp cellar floor. Somewhere between the cabin and Millerstown, he'd transformed from generous lover into hardened FBI agent. They'd situated themselves in the cellar last night, waiting for her mom to show up this morning. All night long he'd rattled off backup plans and more backup plans. He was ready for anything. And so was she. She'd dig her way out of this mess without putting Sean's life in danger. Her plan was under way, as well.

He paused and gripped the railing to the stairs. "Remember, I should talk to her first. She thinks you're dead. You sure she'll even come down here?"

"She has to." She pointed to a bucket of supplies beneath the utility sink.

He started pacing again, raking his hand through his hair.

"Relax, everything will be fine," she said.

"How can you be so calm? You know what they're capable of. They won't stop until they've got what they want."

"Well, they don't know we're here, do they?"

The sound of the door opening upstairs made him freeze in midstep. He put his index finger to his lips and motioned for her to join him beneath the stairs.

She held her breath, her heartbeat pulsing in her ears. How long had it been since she'd seen Mom?

The cellar door opened and the old wood steps creaked with the pressure of footsteps. Annie's eyes burned as she stared through the wooden slats, recognizing her mother's white, crepe-soled shoes as they descended.

Sean stepped into view. "Mrs. Price."

She screamed.

Annie could see Sean, but the wooden railing blocked her mom.

"What are you doing here?" Mom said, breathless.

"I need to talk to you about Annie."

"I don't understand."

Annie couldn't stand it anymore. She stepped out from the stairs. "Mama?"

The older woman blinked twice and reached for the support beam to steady herself. "I've lost my mind."

"It's really me." Annie walked slowly to her mom.

"Annabelle? But how?"

"I'm alive, Mama." She reached out her hand.

"If I touch ya, will ya disappear?"

"No, Mama." She read the shock in her mother's eyes, the disbelief. "I missed you." She touched her mother's sweater.

Margaret Price's legs wobbled and Sean caught her. "Hold on there. Come on, you'd better sit a minute."

He guided her to the stairs and motioned for Annie. She sat beside her mother and brushed a wisp of graying hair from her forehead.

"I've died and gone to heaven. That's what this is," she said. "Must have taken a tumble down these old steps and broke my neck."

"It's really me. I'm okay. I'm alive. You're fine. We're all fine." She glanced at Sean.

He nodded and walked over to the half window

that looked out onto the street. "Is this place rented out, Mrs. Price?"

"No, sir. Not until Friday."

"So we're safe, for now."

She stared into her mom's clear blue eyes, so like her own. "Everything's going to be okay," Annie said. "Sean will make sure everything is okay."

She gave her mom a hug, inhaling the scent of talcum that she knew so well. Her mom hugged her back, tentatively at first, then squeezed, as she had when Annie was a child. Tears watered her eyes.

Annie broke the embrace and smiled.

"You're really here," Mama said. "But, how can this be?" Mama's eyes darted from Annie to Sean and back again.

"It's complicated and I'm still in danger," Annie said. "Bad men are after my research. After the car accident, the FBI kept me hidden. They didn't want the bad men to get me."

"But you didn't tell me—"

"I was unconscious for a long time. Then I woke up and didn't remember anything. Except the sound of your voice."

They hugged and Annie fought off a flood of tears that threatened to escape. "Mama, I love you."

Sean glanced out the window, cataloging the Jeep and maroon Buick parked across the street. He felt like an intruder, listening to sobs of joy of a reunion between mother and child. A reunion he'd never experience.

He closed his eyes on the jagged pain. His mother may not have been able to defend him against the tyrant of a father, but she was still his mother. And she didn't deserve to die at fifty-one.

"How's Crystal?" Annie asked her mom.

"She's got a new job."

"No!" Annie said in disbelief.

"As a computer salesman, I mean woman. She flies all over the country."

As they caught up and as each minute passed, Sean realized how foreign this was to him: family, friends, neighbors who cared about one another. His upbringing had consisted of running and hiding, of making up excuses for teachers but wanting them to guess the real reason he could barely move his arm or the real cause of his black eye.

"And Aunt Jo has taken up in-line skating," Mrs. Price said.

"She's got to be seventy!"

"Seventy-seven," Mrs. Price confirmed.

He didn't belong here with Annie and her sweet mom. He was a beaten dog, trained to be mean. Annie could make him punch as many pillows as she wanted, but it wouldn't change the fact that sooner or later Sean would lose it and attack, like his father.

"I've still got that tea you sent me from London," Mrs. Price said.

"What tea?" Annie questioned.

"The tin of Earl Grey you sent about two weeks

before the accident. You told me to save it for your next visit because it's your favorite. I didn't think you liked tea."

Sean looked at Annie. A puzzled expression creased her brow.

"Annie?"

"I don't like tea, do I?"

"You never drank it around me," he said.

"You couldn't stand the stuff," Mrs. Price said. "Ever since you stayed with Aunt Jo when you were ten and had the flu. Jo, bless her heart, pumped you full of some homemade tea concoction. You wouldn't go near the stuff after that."

"The tin of tea." Annie stood. "That's it! I remember taking the tea bags out—" she mimed the action with her hands "—I slipped a mini hard drive into it." She looked at Sean. "The hard drive must have the formula."

And, he hoped, the accidental recording she'd made of Raymond's plans to release a Level Four virus. Annie didn't understand why he would do that. But Sean did. Raymond planned to drive up the price of the vaccine by releasing the unknown virus.

He'd explained that to Annie that cold February night, but she wouldn't believe him. That's when he spilled the whole truth: he was FBI assigned to expose Raymond any way he could, even if that meant using Annie's feelings to get close to Raymond. Even worse, Raymond had ordered Sean to kill her.

"So, it's almost over," she sighed.

It *was* almost over. This case, their love. He knew once she remembered it all, she'd want no part of him.

And that's as it should be. She'd go home with her mom, settle back in with family and friends in her small farm community and surround herself with people who cared about her.

And he'd get back to business finding a new mark to punish.

"We're going to be okay," she said, wrapping her arms around his neck.

He glanced at her mom, whose disappointed expression didn't surprise him. She could see he was poison. Everyone could see it, except Annie.

"Hang on." He broke the embrace. "We need to figure out how to get the tin without putting you or your mother in danger."

"Let's go get it." She helped her mom to her feet.

"That definitely isn't a good idea," he said. "Your mom should go through her normal workday and go home. We don't want to draw suspicion to her."

"You think people are watching me?" Mrs. Price said.

"Yes, ma'am. I suggest you go about your business, and we'll hook up tomorrow."

She gave him the location of her first job. She hugged Annie one more time.

"I love you, Mama," she whispered.

They held each other for another minute, and then her mom started up the stairs.

The door swung open and Hatch grabbed her, shoving a pistol into her rib cage. "Hello there!"

"Mama!" Annie cried, racing up the steps.

"Annie, no!" Sean called out.

"Stay back," Hatch threatened.

Sean dug his fingers into the stair railing. This was his fault. He hadn't seen it coming. But how?

Another figure stepped into the doorway. Hell. Agent Jackson.

"So, the perfect agent MacNeil really screwed up this time," Jackson said with a smirk.

"Let her go!" Annie said.

"Zip it," Hatch ordered.

Sean analyzed his options. They didn't look good.

"What are you thinking, smart guy?" Hatch said, pulling Annie's mom closer. "You wouldn't be thinking about escaping this little mess you made, would you?"

Sean clenched his fist.

"Now, what should we do with all of you?" Hatch said. "All I really need is the brainy lady there."

"Let them go," a voice said from behind Hatch.

Hatch did as ordered and raised his hands. Jackson did the same. They moved out of view and another form filled the doorway.

Sean's blood ran cold.

"Raymond!" Annie cried. "You came!"

Chapter Thirteen

"You called him?" Rage burned in Sean's gut.

"We needed help," she said. "Raymond has always taken care of me."

"And that I have." He smirked at Sean.

Damn, Sean should have told her the whole story, regardless of what she'd think of him. At least that way she'd know Phelps was not her savior.

She started up the stairs, such trust in her eyes. Sean wanted to rip something apart with his bare hands. How could it have come to this? Annie trusting her enemy, the man who'd ordered her death?

"Annie," Sean said.

"It's okay," she said.

"Come on, Mama. We're safe."

Annie took her mom's arm. Margaret Price glanced at Sean. She knew something wasn't right.

Sean followed the group upstairs where Phelps locked Hatch and Jackson in a hall closet. Sean didn't buy it. He knew Hatch and Jackson were looking for him. This had to be a show for Annie, to keep up his "good guy" image.

"This is far too complicated for the local authorities, wouldn't you agree, Agent MacNeil?" Phelps said.

So, Phelps knew he was FBI. What was he going to do about it?

"Calling the locals would only confuse things," Sean agreed.

"Please sit. I'm desperate to know how you managed to find my Annie and take care of her all these months when I thought her dead. I'm in your debt." Raymond motioned with his gun for him to sit down. Settling her mom on the couch, Annie didn't notice the subtle threat.

"I'd be dead if it weren't for Sean," Annie said. "Bad men are after me, Raymond. They want my research."

"And Agent MacNeil. What does he want?"

"He's been protecting me." She glanced at Sean. Sean sat across the room from Annie.

Raymond positioned himself in a leather wingback chair, resting the gun on his knee. "I think the best thing for everyone is if I take Annie home. You must have been through such an ordeal, child."

"I'm okay, thanks to Sean."

She smiled at Sean and the gratitude in her eyes wasn't lost on Raymond.

"Yes, well, I'm sure he did a splendid job. But then that's what he gets paid to do. You're safe now. I'm here to make everything right. I need you to put the final touches on the vaccine. You told me it was ready, but I've had it tested and it isn't effective. I'll take you home and you can get right to work."

"But I'm not going home with you," she said.

Silence blanketed the room.

"Annie, that's where you belong," Raymond said. "You're special. No one in the outside world understands you the way I do."

"I'm twenty-seven. I should have a life of my own."

"No, child," Raymond scolded. "You don't have the ability to function in the real world. That's why I've taken care of you all these years. You're different. You don't belong out there."

"You're wrong." She stood and paced to the window. "In the last few days, I've learned a lot about myself. I may not remember everything about my life before, about the accident…" Her voice trailed off. She turned and squared off at Raymond. "But I remember feeling lonely. I shouldn't feel lonely, Raymond. I should have friends, I should be able to spend more time with Mom and my sisters and their kids."

"It's been over a year since you've seen Cindy and the twins," Mrs. Price offered.

"That's not right," Annie said, sitting next to her mother, then looking at Raymond. "I'm sure you had my best interest at heart, but that's over now. I might be smarter than most, but I'm still a human being. I have feelings and needs that I can't satisfy by hiding out in your mansion."

Sean marveled at the new Annie, the strong-willed, determined young woman who was finally standing up for herself.

"I suppose this is your doing," Raymond said to Sean.

Sean cocked his head to one side, as if he hadn't a clue what Raymond was referring to. He couldn't let the bastard know how important Annie was to him, or Phelps would use it against him.

"Annie, this is unacceptable. You must come home and finish your research."

But according to Annie, her research was finished. Did that mean she didn't trust him?

Sean could only hope.

Raymond got up and paced to the sofa, towering over Annie and her mom. "Your mother can even come stay for a few weeks. She could have the guest quarters. It will be like a family reunion."

Sean focused on how to turn the situation around, how to subdue Phelps without upsetting Annie, and without the gun that Phelps casually held in his hand going off. Sean stood and took a step toward the sofa.

"Stay where you are, MacNeil," Phelps ordered, but didn't aim the gun at him. Not yet. He was still playing "nice Raymond" for Annie's sake.

"Annie?" Raymond said. "My home is where you belong."

"I'm an adult, Raymond. I should be living on my own."

"Mrs. Price, talk to your daughter." Raymond pulled Annie's mom to her feet with a grip of her elbow. "Tell her how important it is to come stay with me."

Raymond's words reverberated in Annie's brain. She'd heard them before, years ago. He'd said them when he came to visit the farm for the third time, the day he took her home with him.

Her eyes caught on Raymond's hand, squeezing Mama's arm. Sharp, bright memories flashed to the surface. Praising her, then belittling her. She'd thought it a normal childhood, but as she grew older she wondered. Then she'd met Sean and felt true love for the first time.

Raymond didn't love her. He wanted Annie for her research. She remembered something about the farm, it was failing and…

"You bought me," she whispered.

Raymond glanced at her.

"You bought me and took me away from my mother and sisters when I needed them more than anything."

"You needed to hone that brilliant mind of yours. Your mother knew it, just as I did."

"You threatened…what was it? To take the farm?"

"You remember it backward, my dear. I offered your mother to pay the mortgage on the farm in exchange for educating you. Seems like an unfair deal for me, but I'm the philanthropic type. I sacrificed thousands of dollars so your family could keep their precious spot of land. I had to clothe and feed you. Pay for tutors and friends."

"You paid for my friends?" She felt as if she'd been punched.

"There were no other children in my house. You needed playmates."

"You took care of me."

"Very good care."

But that's not how she remembered it. Assaulted by memories, she took a deep breath, a part of her wanting to fight them off, another part wanting the truth.

In the lab…accidentally recording a conversation between Raymond and a stranger. They planned to unleash a virus. She didn't understand. Must talk to Sean. He'd explain things. But Sean was…ordered to kill her? No, she wouldn't believe it. He'd been pretending to love her, when all the time he was FBI, working undercover as her bodyguard. Now her guardian had ordered him to kill her.

Must take off, get away. Driving very fast. She'd only driven a few times. Wasn't skilled. Didn't matter. Had to get away. Heart aching with betrayal…the two men who were supposed to care for her most in the world had used her.

Not worthy of love. Tears streaming down her face. A sharp turn—

"Mama," she whispered.

Mama squeezed Annie's hand, bringing her back to earth.

What a fool she'd been—Raymond was the enemy, not her protector. But she'd wanted so desperately to believe that someone truly loved her for herself, not for her brains.

Her gaze caught Sean's green eyes. He'd used her, too, but not now. Now there was more. She knew it in her heart. And his life depended on her next move.

She placed her arm around her mother. "I'd like to stay with Mama for a few days." Lame, but worth a try.

Raymond sighed and let go of Mama's arm. "I'm sorry, Annie. That's not acceptable."

He went to the hallway closet and opened the door. Sean lunged at him. "Annie, run! Get out of here."

With an arm around Mama, she raced toward the front door.

"I'll kill him," Raymond threatened.

Annie froze, afraid to turn around.

"Help me with him," Raymond ordered.

She spun around to see Sean pinned to the floor by Hatch. Jackson stood by with a satisfied grin on his face.

Of course, they were all Raymond's men: Zinkerman, Hatch, Jackson. And Raymond always got what he wanted.

"You're coming with me until you finish what you started," Raymond said. "If I'm to unleash the Influx Virus, I need to have the vaccine to cure it."

She held her mom closer. "Why?"

"For a smart girl, you're so naive. I thought you'd finished the formula, but I was wrong. Something didn't feel right about your death so I hired a team of investigators and found you at Appleton. I sent my man to assess the situation and decided it best to treat you there because we didn't know who we were dealing with. FBI, incompetent, bumbling idiots."

Hatch kicked Sean in the ribs and he grunted.

"Zinkerman, that fool. His associate nearly killed you, then they both let you slip through their fingers. They had to pay for their incompetence."

Annie swallowed hard. "You had Dr. Zinkerman killed."

"Insignificant man. Like MacNeil. A thorn in my side." Raymond knelt down and trailed the gun along Sean's jawline.

"Stop it! Sean, I'm sorry. I didn't remember," she cried.

"Enough!" Raymond shouted. "What's the matter with you? This man manipulated you, used you to slake his lust over and over again, and you care about him? He's only in this for the job. He used you once and he's using you now. At least I'm honest about what I want."

"You don't know what you're talking about. Sean, tell him he's wrong."

"Silly girl," Raymond said.

She didn't move, waiting for Sean to defend himself. His eyes burned fire at Raymond.

"Sean?"

He shot her a cold, steely glare that froze her heart. It was as if he wasn't there anymore, as if the kind, gentle man she'd loved somehow had vacated his body.

"Get her out of here," Raymond ordered.

Jackson started toward Annie and her mom.

"I love you, Annie."

Sean's words stopped her cold. She turned and studied his eyes, eyes filled with love, drenched in guilt.

Hatch kicked him in the stomach, and Sean rolled onto his side with a moan.

You're smart, Annie. You can figure out a solution to anything.

The words that had been both a blessing and a curse rang in her ears. She had to buy time. If she angered Raymond further, he might shoot Mama, or Sean, or both.

Buy time. Think your way out of this.

"You'll let Mom go after I finish the formula?" she said.

Raymond smiled "You have my word."

Like hell.

"What about Sean? You'll release him if I leave with you?"

"I'll do even better. We'll keep him at the mansion for personal recreation."

Did he mean hers or his?

"It could take months to finish," she said.

"Let's not play games. You told me you were

finished and I believed you." He took three steps toward her. "It's time to come home."

Sean looked at her with such defeat in his eyes.

"No games, Raymond. Just–" she hesitated "—instinct."

Adrenaline shot through her body as she shoved Mama aside and shouldered Raymond in the stomach. He stumbled backward into the wall, and the gun went flying.

"Nnnnnoooo!"

Annie was shoved out of the way as Sean punched Hatch in the gut, then shoved him through the screen door. With seemingly superhuman strength, Sean grabbed Raymond and tossed him onto the porch like a rag doll. He grabbed Jackson, who whimpered and held his hands to his face.

Sean released him. "You're not worth it."

He took Jackson's gun, then stormed out onto the porch. Annie watched the man she loved pistol-whip Hatch into submission. Raymond tried to escape, but Sean tackled him and grabbed him by the lapels.

"You're not going anywhere." He slammed Raymond's head against the porch, grunting a low, violent sound that shot goose bumps down her spine. She could feel the anger, rage and hatred emanating from his body. Raymond swung blindly, and Sean slugged him in the face. Raymond went still.

"Annie?" Mama said, fear lacing her voice.

"It's okay, Mom."

She went to him and touched his shoulder. "Sean?"

He looked up and blinked twice, as if trying to figure out where he was and what he was doing.

"It's okay now," she said. "They can't hurt us."

He glanced at the men, then at his bloodied hand. Annie thought she heard a sob rack his chest.

He placed a closed fist to his mouth and sat there for a few seconds. Clearing his throat, he stood.

"I'd better call in." He pulled out his cell.

She stared at him, wondering what self-torture he put himself through for losing control and saving her life. She knew Sean better than she knew herself. The pain and self-deprecation in his eyes nearly tore her apart. She knew what was coming next. Self-condemnation, guilt, shame.

Hadn't he had enough of that in one lifetime?

As she calmed Mama, two squad cars pulled up. Oh, great. They were going to arrest her.

A patrolman got out of his car. "You MacNeil?"

"Yes." Sean went to the officer and explained the situation, then returned to Annie. "Connors called the local cops to take Phelps and his men to jail. The other officer will take you back to your mom's."

"Sean." She touched his arm.

He pulled away. "I've gotta wash up." He glanced at his hands, then disappeared into the house.

Sean was desperate to get away from her, from

this whole damned scene. Of all the places to snap, he had to do it in front of the woman he loved.

The woman he loved. Well, if he loved her all that much, he'd disappear from her life for good this time.

He made his way to the bathroom without Annie finding him. The best thing she could do is leave him alone, walk off into her new life and forget the goodbyes, the apologies. But then she had nothing to be sorry about. Not like Sean.

He stood in the small powder room and rinsed off his hands. The commotion of agents echoed down the hall from the living room. They were questioning Annie and her mom. How much would she tell? Would she confess that she and Sean had made love?

It didn't matter. Right now, all that mattered was getting away. From this place, from Annie, from the ghosts that hounded him.

He glanced into the mirror and spotted Annie's compassionate expression behind him.

"How are you?" she asked.

"Fine."

"No, you're not." She stepped inside the bathroom and closed the door.

He ripped his gaze from hers and continued washing his hands.

"Sean—"

"Annie, don't." He shut off the faucet and grabbed a towel. "Look, this didn't happen. We were never real. I've accomplished my job and now you can get on with your life."

He reached around her for the door. She blocked it with her body.

"Please move." He didn't know how much more of this he could take.

"I'm not going anywhere until you listen to what I have to say."

He braced himself.

"I want you to grow up," she said. "Forget this stupid notion that you're like your dad, and live for yourself. I love you Sean, and I know you love me."

"Use your head, Annie. You saw what I did out there. I'm an animal."

"Get off the pity pot. You've been on it long enough."

"Excuse me?"

"You're not your father. What you did for Mom and me is what any normal, red-blooded man would do to protect the people he loves. And you love me, Sean. I know you do because you became your worst nightmare to protect me. Can't you see that?"

"All I see is how many ways I can hurt you."

"Think about this," she said. "I taunted you at the cabin, got in your face and wouldn't let up, but did you hurt me? Did you lose it and come after me like your father came after your mother? No, because you're not him. You're a wonderful, caring, generous man."

"And you're a naive scientist."

Her breath caught as if he'd slapped her.

"I've said what I needed to say." She pushed up on tiptoe and kissed his cheek, her breath warming his skin like sunshine on a hot summer's day. "I love you."

She turned and ran down the hall.

"You really are a bastard," he whispered.

And she deserved better.

Chapter Fourteen

Sitting in the den, Annie studied the family photo album and smiled at the picture of her milking Hennie the cow for the first time. She was only six.

But she didn't have to study the worn, yellowed pages for help. She remembered. All of it.

Sometimes she wished she hadn't. She remembered she'd lost years of her life to her own naiveté, trusting a man who only wanted her for her brilliant mind, namely for the vaccine that he could use to hold the world hostage.

She was a one-dimensional scientist, obsessed with her work, a naive farm girl with an overactive brain.

No wonder Sean didn't love her.

"Argh!" She jumped to her feet and marched into the kitchen.

"Hungry?" her mom said, wrapping a loaf of bread for the neighbors.

"Kinda." She sat at the kitchen table.

Mom grabbed the ceramic pig cookie jar and

plopped it in front of her, then poured a glass of milk. "You'll be okay while I'm gone?"

"I'll be fine." She tapped her fingers to the table.

"Love you." Her mom placed a kiss atop her head, and Annie smiled back at her.

"Love you, too."

Her mom grabbed the bread and left.

Annie needed a little alone time. The farm had been swarmed by locals for the past few weeks, well-wishers and those curious about their hometown celebrity genius.

But the only thing Annie was curious about was what had happened to Agent Sean MacNeil. To think she could develop a vaccine for a deadly virus, but she couldn't heal one man's soul.

"Some genius," she muttered.

Then again, he was so damn stubborn. Determined to keep anyone and everyone out of his heart. Mulling over that scene at Pinewood, she figured out that he was protecting her, driving her away for fear he'd hurt her.

Hogwash. He was a typical male who'd acted in a completely justified manner when he gone after Raymond.

She dunked an oatmeal cookie, more convinced than ever that Sean did, in fact, love her. If only he could let go of the shame he wore like blinders, he could see the truth. But nothing she said or did would open his eyes. He'd have to learn that lesson himself.

She suspected he wasn't all that great a student, at least not when it came to forgiving himself.

The front door creaked open.

"Mama?" Annie called.

"You wouldn't believe who I found coming up the drive."

God, not more visitors.

She popped the cookie in her mouth and turned. She froze in midchew. Sean. Dressed in tight-fitting jeans, a navy blue FBI T-shirt and cowboy boots, he looked even better than she remembered.

"Hi," he said, shoving his hands into his jeans pockets.

She moved her jaw, trying to finish the cookie so she could speak.

"Not talking to me, huh?" he said.

Putting out her finger, she took a sip of milk and swallowed. "I was eating a cookie."

"What kind?"

"What?" she said, shocked that he was standing in the kitchen doorway.

"What kind of cookie?"

"Oatmeal raisin."

"My favorite."

He smiled, and she thought she'd cry.

"Sean, have a seat. We've got lots of cookies." Mama gave him a nudge from behind, and he sat at the table across from Annie. Mom smiled and disappeared down the hall.

Annie found herself alone with Sean. Then a horrible thought seized her.

"Is this a follow-up visit?" she asked.

He grabbed a cookie from the jar. "I'm on vacation. Thought I should stop by."

"Oh." That didn't really answer her question. "Let me guess, you brought divorce papers?" The words tasted bitter on her tongue.

"Since your signature was forged the marriage isn't—" he hesitated "—real." He placed his cookie to the table and traced his finger around it. That simple but familiar movement made her breasts feel heavy with wanting.

"I really screwed up, didn't I?" he said.

"That depends." She leaned back and crossed her arms over her chest. "Are you here to close the case or kiss me?"

"What?" he glanced up.

"I love you. No formulas, no research, no equations. Just love."

Sean took a deep breath. She really loved him. She'd said as much at Pinewood, but he couldn't believe her through the haze of shame.

"I don't know why." She stood and paced to the window overlooking the farm. "You're a jerk. You married me against my will, used physical intimidation more than once, told me you didn't care about me and dyed my hair orange."

"I'm sorry," he said, wishing for better words, healing words.

"I've forgiven you for most of it, but the hair? Do you know I've tried three rinses and none of them worked? I'll have to make a trip to Lucy's Luscious Locks two towns over. They're experts at—"

"You've...forgiven me?" he said.

"Except for the hair. You're going to have to do something pretty amazing to make up for that."

"Annie." In three strides he was holding her, his lips brushing against her delicious orange hair. She loved him. All the gut-wrenching pain seemed to dissolve at the thought of living his life with this incredible woman.

"I don't deserve you," he mumbled into her hair.

"You're right, so I've got a proposition for you."

"What?" He leaned back to look at her. He trailed a strand of neon hair from her cheek. Touching her skin, her beautiful, sweet skin, humbled him in a way like never before.

"I have lots of experiments planned for the next sixty or so years and I need a human guinea pig, someone about six foot, two hundred pounds...with very, soft lips." She pulled his mouth to hers. The kiss was tender and sweet.

And simply perfect.

She broke the kiss and gazed into his eyes. "Bottom line? We belong together, Agent MacNeil."

"You are one smart woman, Annie Price."

He sealed her offer with a kiss and wondered what experiments she had in mind.

* * * * *

Set in darkness beyond the ordinary world.
Passionate tales of life and death.
With characters' lives ruled by laws the everyday
world can't begin to imagine.

Introducing NOCTURNE, a spine-tingling
new line from Silhouette Books.

The thrills and chills begin with UNFORGIVEN
by Lindsay McKenna.

Plucked from the depths of hell, former military
sharpshooter Reno Manchahi was hired by the government to kill a thief, but he had a mission of his
own. Descended from a family of shape-shifters,
Reno vowed to get the revenge he'd thirsted for all
these years. But his mission went awry when his
target turned out to be a powerful seductress, Mag-
dalena Calen Hernandez, who risked everything to
battle a potent evil. Suddenly, Reno had to transform
himself into a true hero and fight the enemy that
threatened them all. He had to become a Warrior for
the Light....

Turn the page for a sneak preview of
UNFORGIVEN by Lindsay McKenna.
On sale September 26 wherever books are sold.

Chapter 1

One shot...one kill.

The sixteen-pound sledgehammer came down with such fierce power that the granite boulder shattered instantly. A spray of glittering mica exploded into the air and sparkled momentarily around the man who wielded the tool as if it were a weapon. Sweat ran in rivulets down Reno Manchahi's drawn, intense face. Naked from the waist up, the hot July sun beating down on his back, he hefted the sledgehammer skyward once more. Muscles in his thick forearms leaped and biceps bulged. Even his breath was focused on the boulder. In his mind's eye, he pictured Army General Robert Hampton's fleshy, arrogant fifty-year-old features on the rock's surface. Air exploded from between his lips as he brought the avenging hammer down. The boulder pulverized beneath his funneled hatred.

One shot...one kill...

Nostrils flaring, he inhaled the dank, humid heat and drew it deep into his massive lungs. Revenge allowed Reno to endure his imprisonment at a U.S. Navy brig near San Diego, California. Drops of sweat were flung in all directions as the crack of his sledgehammer claimed a third stone victim. Mouth taut, Reno moved to the next boulder.

The other prisoners in the stone yard gave him a wide berth. They always did. They instinctively felt his simmering hatred, the palpable revenge in his cinnamon-colored eyes, was more than skin-deep.

And they whispered he was different.

Reno enjoyed being a loner for good reason. He came from a medicine family of shape-shifters. But even this secret power had not protected him—or his family. His wife, Ilona, and his three-year-old daughter, Sarah, were dead. Murdered by Army General Hampton in their former home on USMC base in Camp Pendleton, California. Bitterness thrummed through Reno as he savagely pushed the toe of his scarred leather boot against several smaller pieces of gray granite that were in his way.

The sun beat down upon Manchahi's naked shoulders, grown dark red over time, shouting his half-

Apache heritage. With his straight black hair grazing his thick shoulders, copper skin and broad face with high cheekbones, everyone knew he was Indian. When he'd first arrived at the brig, some of the prisoners taunted him and called him Geronimo. Something strange happened to Reno during his fight with the name-calling prisoners. Leaning down after he'd won the scuffle, he'd snarled into each of their bloodied faces that if they were going to call him anything, they would call him *gan,* which was the Apache word for *devil.*

His attackers had been shocked by the wounds on their faces, the deep claw marks. Reno recalled doubling his fist as they'd attacked him en masse. In that split second, he'd gone into an altered state of consciousness. In times of danger, he transformed into a jaguar. A deep, growling sound had emitted from his throat as he defended himself in the three-against-one fracas. It all happened so fast that he thought he had imagined it. He'd seen his hands morph into a forearm and paw, claws extended. The slashes left on the three men's faces after the fight told him he'd begun to shape-shift. A fist made bruises and swelling; not four perfect, deep claw marks. Stunned and anxious, he hid the knowledge of what else he was from these prisoners. Reno's only defense was to make all the prisoners so damned scared of him and remain a loner.

Alone. Yeah, he was alone, all right. The steel

hammer swept downward with hellish ferocity. As the granite groaned in protest, Reno shut his eyes for just a moment. Sweat dripped off his nose and square chin.

Straightening, he wiped his furrowed, wet brow and looked into the pale blue sky. What got his attention was the startling cry of a red-tailed hawk as it flew over the brig yard. Squinting, he watched the bird. Reno could make out the rust-colored tail on the hawk. As a kid growing up on the Apache reservation in Arizona, Reno knew that all animals that appeared before him were messengers.

Brother, what message do you bring me? Reno knew one had to ask in order to receive. Allowing the sledgehammer to drop to his side, he concentrated on the hawk who wheeled in tightening circles above him.

Freedom! the hawk cried in return.

Reno shook his head, his black hair moving against his broad, thickset shoulders. *Freedom? No way, Brother. No way.* Figuring that he was making up the hawk's shrill message, Reno turned away. Back to his rocks. Back to picturing Hampton's smug face.

Freedom!

* * * * *

Look for UNFORGIVEN by Lindsay McKenna,
the spine-tingling launch title from
Silhouette Nocturne™.
Available September 26 wherever books are sold.

Silhouette®

nocturne™

Save $1.⁰⁰ off

your purchase of any Silhouette® Nocturne™ novel.

Receive $1.00 off

any Silhouette® Nocturne™ novel.

Available wherever books are sold, including most bookstores, supermarkets, drugstores and discount stores.

Coupon expires December 1, 2006. Redeemable at participating retail outlets in the U.S. only. Limit one coupon per customer.

RETAILER: Harlequin Enterprises Ltd. will pay the face value of this coupon plus 8¢ if submitted by the customer for this specified product only. Any other use constitutes fraud. Coupon is nonassignable. Void if taxed, prohibited or restricted by law. Void if copied. Consumer must pay for any government taxes. Mail to Harlequin Enterprises Ltd., P.O. Box 880478, El Paso, TX 88588-0478, U.S.A. Cash value 1/100 cents. Limit one coupon per customer. Valid in the U.S. only.

5 65373 00076 2   (8100) 0 11265

SNCOUPUS

Silhouette

nocturne™

Save $1.⁰⁰ off

your purchase of any
Silhouette® Nocturne™ novel.

Receive $1.00 off
any Silhouette® Nocturne™ novel.

**Available wherever books are sold, including most
bookstores, supermarkets, drugstores and discount stores.**

Coupon expires December 1, 2006. Redeemable at participating
retail outlets in Canada only. Limit one coupon per customer.

RETAILER: Harlequin Enterprises Limited will pay the face value of this coupon
plus 10.25 cents if submitted by the customer for this specified product only. Any
other use constitutes fraud. Coupon is nonassignable. Void if taxed, prohibited or
restricted by law. Consumer must pay any government taxes. Mail to Harlequin
Enterprises Ltd., P.O. Box 3000, Saint John, New Brunswick E2L 4L3, Canada. Limit
one coupon per customer. Valid in Canada only.

52607136

SNCOUPCDN

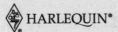
HARLEQUIN®

INTRIGUE

COMING NEXT MONTH

#945 RED ALERT by Jessica Andersen
Corporate mogul Erik Falco is drawn to acquiring a new medical breakthrough from Boston General Hospital before his competitors. But could Dr. Megan Corning also be part of the deal?

#946 CHAIN REACTION by Rebecca York
Security Breach
When an explosion exposes Gage Darnell to a dangerous chemical, he discovers he's acquired the ability to manipulate matter with his mind. But on the run and looking to reconnect with his estranged wife, Lily, will he be powerless to change hers?

#947 BABY JANE DOE by Julie Miller
The Precinct
An unsolvable case. An I.A. investigator with a keen mind to keep their public love private. And a vicious stalker with all the answers. All in a day's work for KCPD commissioner Shauna Cartwright.

#948 FOOTPRINTS IN THE SNOW by Cassie Miles
He's a Mystery
When a freak blizzard delivers Shana Parisi into the arms of sergeant Luke Rawlins, she's swept into a secret mission of the utmost importance and a love that transcends time.

#949 ISLAND IN THE FOG by Leona Karr
Eclipse
Searching for her missing sister on Greystone Island, Ashley Davis finds herself side by side with police officer Brad Taylor, who's investigating multiple deaths in the wealthy Langdon family. The family her sister worked for.

#950 COVERT CONCEPTION by Delores Fossen
Neither Rick Gravari nor Natalie Sinclair knew they were part of an experiment to produce genetically improved babies until Natalie unexpectedly becomes pregnant. But even if these rivals unveil this vast conspiracy, can they become the perfect parents?